By Graham Thomas
Published by Ivy Books:

MALICE IN THE HIGHLANDS
MALICE IN CORNWALL

MALICE IN CORNWALL

Graham Thomas

IVY BOOKS • NEW YORK

For Becky, Graham, and Laura.
With thanks to Wendy Hindle
and to Mr. Alan Harvey of
Constantine Bay, Cornwall

In my seashaken house
On a breakneck of rocks . . .
Out there, crow black, men
Tackled with clouds

DYLAN THOMAS,
Author's Prologue, *Collected Poems 1934–1952*

PROLOGUE

The moon was large that night and so was she. She had left her friends in the pub and set out alone along the beach humming the latest Beatles tune to herself. The lights of the pub and the din of revelry—snatches of laughter, the faint tintinnabulation of clinking glasses on the patio, and the beat of the music—dwindling in the distance. She thought about her boyfriend back there drinking himself into a stupor. Their romantic weekend at the seaside hadn't exactly turned out that way; he'd be no good at all to her later, but then he wasn't much good at the best of times, and she wasn't into alcohol. Screw *him*, she was having a gas!

She kicked off her shoes and ran along the beach, heart pounding and the air rushing into her open mouth. Her long hair flew behind her like a white mare's tail in the moonlight. She experienced the sharp texture of sand beneath her feet, the cooling breeze against her skin, the iodine smell of the sea. She spread her arms wide, shafts of golden light emanating from her fingertips, encircling the moon with a writing aurora. "God, I'm stoned!" she shouted to anyone who cared to listen.

The sea whispered to her, drawing her closer to the water's edge. The sand had given way to shingle, so she slowed, prancing gingerly amongst the stones; patches of slimy sea wrack squished between her toes and she wished that she had kept her shoes. Her eyes widened. The beach was moving as if a million chitinous creatures were swarming over it and there was an acrid smell in the air. I mustn't freak, she told herself.

She stared in wonder at her body; it was bathed in a suffusive light that seemed to originate beneath her skin, perhaps from the intricate pattern of blue-wire veins she could trace with her finger. The light expanded around her, and she was no longer sure what was inside or outside or whether the distinction even had any meaning.

The waves hissed and clawed at the rocks with white-foam fingers. She could sense the rise and fall of luminous seaweed in the bay and cold eyes searching the deeps. She knew then that she was not alone.

She couldn't understand why she hadn't noticed it before. Shimmering in the moonlight like a fantastic mirror, a large pool filled by the rising tide was now isolated by a circle of rocks jutting up like broken black teeth. She felt as if she were floating above its quicksilver surface. She tried to focus at a point beyond her reflection to see what lay at the heart of it. There was something there, just beyond the limits of her perception, something elusive, ethereal, yet deeply meaningful and transcendent.

After what seemed like hours, an image slowly began to resolve itself beneath the surface of the water. A young girl, perhaps sixteen or seventeen, stared back at her with incredulous eyes, pupils dilated like her own, skin like alabaster, a cloud of dark hair drifting around her face as if softly stirred by her breath. Except how could the girl be breathing?

I'm really tripping now, she thought wonderingly. She moved closer. The girl in the pool was naked, like some lovely mermaid, wearing only a choker, a black satin ribbon encircling her slender neck with an ivory cameo in the center.

She stared at this simple if incongruous adornment, fascinated. The choker was oddly frayed at the edges, and it occurred to her that something was not quite right. She was coming down fast.

She suddenly realized that it wasn't a choker at all, but rather a deep dark gash, the severed trachea exposed like some obscene white hosepipe. The throat had been neatly cut.

They could hear her screaming all the way back at the pub.

CHAPTER 1

Detective-Sergeant William Black slowly mounted the steps of his semidetached house, critically surveying the general state of disrepair. His brow furrowed as he compiled a mental list of the items needing attention, just as he had every day for the past month or so. It was a sad litany of neglect: the rusting wrought-iron railings and the sagging drainpipe, not to mention the peeling paintwork around the door. He really must get on with it, for he knew better than most that little jobs neglected had a habit of becoming big jobs. Tomorrow was his day off, right enough, but he needed to catch up on his reading, and hadn't Muriel said something about the kids coming over? He shook his head sadly. He prided himself on being handy around the house, but between the grandchildren and his studies there hadn't been much spare time lately.

He hung his mac on the coatrack in the hallway and looked into the sitting room. He could hear Muriel hoovering upstairs. The mantel clock was striking six. He consulted his watch and then walked over to the mantelpiece, opened the little glass window on the clock, and moved the minute hand ahead three minutes. Satisfied, he went into the kitchen and out the back door to fetch a cool bottle of ale from the garden shed. He returned to the sitting room, dislodged the cat from his favorite chair, settled himself with a contented sigh, and began reading a dog-eared copy of *King Lear*.

Muriel came down the stairs a few minutes later lugging the vacuum, the hose draped over her shoulder like Captain Nemo, Black fancied, entwined with a giant squid.

"Evenin', love," he rumbled affectionately.

"I didn't hear you come in."

"Anything I can do?"

"There's a shepherd's pie in the oven."

"Her voice was ever soft, gentle and low—an excellent thing in woman."

She smiled indulgently. "Enjoy the peace and quiet while you can. I've got a list of things for you to mend after supper."

"Like the Bard said, I will leave no rubs nor botches in the work."

"Oh, Bill!"

He had become incorrigible since he'd enrolled in that adult education course at the local college last year. When she'd brought home the syllabi, Adventures in English Literature was the last thing she'd had in mind. Weaving or Beginning Pottery for her, and perhaps Roof Repair or Advanced Plumbing for him, something to help fill their evenings, but never just reading. Not that she had anything against reading. She enjoyed a good Jeffrey

Archer as much as anyone, but Bill was—well, so practical and not at all romantic. Not that he wasn't sharp.
You had to be to work on murder cases. But he'd never
shown any inclination to read books before, his cultural
universe having been largely circumscribed by the *Daily
Telegraph* and the telly.

As she busied herself in the kitchen she wondered if
her husband's newly found interest wasn't a symptom of
something deeper, even though he was past the age when
one usually expected that sort of thing. Still, she had
often wondered if he was truly happy with their life
together. They seldom talked about it and she had no
reason to think otherwise, but his tendency to immerse
himself in a new hobby every couple of years, as if to fill
a void, made her wonder. The last time it had been
fishing, not your game fishing—he couldn't afford that,
of course—but coarse fishing. It had begun when Mr.
Powell gave them a salmon, and for over a year it was all
roach and perch, boilies and maggots. This time it was
English literature, and she had to admit that he'd taken to
the subject like nothing else before. He always seemed to
have his nose buried in a book; novels, literary biogra-
phies, poetry—she hardly knew what to expect next. The
odd thing was, up until now, he'd never shown the
slightest inclination to further his education. It was too
late to help him in his career, so she had to assume that it
was purely for personal fulfillment. When pressed, he
joked self-consciously that in order to stay young one
had to stretch the mind to its limits.

She considered herself lucky. Bill was a kind and
attentive husband, a good father and grandfather; she was
proud that he wanted to better himself. And perhaps his

newfound interest in culture would extend to taking her to see a play or a concert occasionally. Visions of *The Phantom* and *Les Mis* danced fleetingly in her head. But then she frowned slightly. If only he would refrain from spouting literary quotations at every available opportunity. It was beginning to get on her nerves.

After supper, they sat cocooned together in comfortable silence, she busy with her knitting and he, having put his Shakespeare aside for the moment, reading the newspaper.

A story buried in the back pages caught his attention. "Here, love, listen to this—the headline says 'The Riddle of Penrick':

For nearly two weeks the residents of the seaside village of Penrick on the north coast of Cornwall have reported seeing a mysterious apparition on the Penrick Sands, a popular summer bathing beach. The Riddle, as it has become known, is said to give off an unearthly light and has been variously described by witnesses as a headless female figure, or as half-animal and half-human. Concern has been expressed by a local councillor, who wishes to remain anonymous, that tourism could be adversely affected. According to a police spokesperson in Camborne, there is no doubt a logical explanation for the reported sightings, although none was given.

What do you think of that?" He chuckled, not envying the police spokesperson. In such cases, you were damned if you said anything and damned if you didn't.

"It sounds a bit far-fetched."

Black smiled knowingly. *"There are more things in heaven and earth,* dear Muriel, *than are dreamt of in your philosophy."*

She was about to reply when the telephone jangled. She handed over the receiver, a strange expression on her face. "It's for you, Bill. It's Mr. Powell."

After he'd rung off, he turned to his wife with that familiar look in his eye. "Well, that's it, love. I'm off again."

Powell replaced the receiver and went back to his table near the front window of the K2 Tandoori Restaurant. The atmosphere was fragrant with spices and a raga played softly in the background. There were numerous plants in large brass pots; the red flock walls were hung with provocative batiks of the Omar Khayyám school; and on the back wall a giant silhouette of the Taj Mahal was painted, with the swinging doors to the kitchen opening in the center of the palace. The only apparent nod to the restaurant's namesake, and a useful deterrent when the lads came in for a riot after the pubs closed, was an ice ax hanging behind the bar.

It was early yet for the dinner crowd, and only two of the other tables were occupied. Powell preferred to come when it was quiet and his old friend Rashid Jamal, the proprietor, wouldn't be too busy for a chat. Powell placed a high value on his friendship with the dapper Pakistani—on more than one occasion a sensible word or a sympathetic ear from Rashid had set him on the right course—not to mention the fact that Rashid served the best curry in London, a considerable accomplishment in a city with more than two thousand Indian restaurants. Powell's wife,

Marion, accompanied him occasionally, although not as often as in the old days when Rashid's wife, Nindi, had presided over the kitchen. Usually he came alone on evenings when he had to work late. Tomorrow he was off to Cornwall to start a new case, and Marion was away for a fortnight in Canada with the boys, so a meal at the K2 had seemed like just the thing.

The K2 Tandoori was for Powell an oasis of tranquillity and sensory delight, as effectively isolated from the outside world and its concerns as if by the eternal snows of the high Karakoram. A couple of hours in the care of Rashid and he generally felt like a new man. Along these lines, he had recently read an article in the *New Scientist* about the addictive qualities of curry. It seems that the active ingredient of hot chilies, capsaicin, triggers the release of endorphins, the body's natural painkillers, creating a sense of pleasure and well-being. The food seems more highly flavored and the experience of eating is intensified. Now with a legitimate excuse for indulging his weakness, Powell was happy to admit that he was basically on the same plane as your garden-variety drug addict. Returning to his newspaper, he munched contentedly on a peppery *pappadam*.

A familiar voice roused him from his reverie. "Erskine, my dear chap, did you get through to your colleague?" Rashid bore a fresh pint of lager for Powell and a lemon squash for himself.

"I managed to catch him in, thanks." Powell cleared away his paper to make room.

Rashid sat down and sighed heavily. "Things are difficult, my friend. I lost my best waiter last week and you cannot imagine how difficult it is to get help that you can rely upon these days."

"I was wondering where Ali was. What happened?" The portly server had been a fixture at the restaurant for several years.

"He took a job at a hotel in Oxford Street. He said he wanted to make a career for himself in the hospitality industry." Rashid looked around sadly. "What does he think this place is—a bloody ironmongers' shop?"

"I read somewhere that the average young person starting out today will change careers four or five times during his or her lifetime," Powell observed neutrally.

But Rashid was not to be so easily distracted. "It is very sad, Erskine. How can one perfect one's craft, one's art, if one is all the time hopping willy-nilly from one frying pan to another? Never trust a tiger who changes his spots, my friend."

Powell bit his tongue and nodded sympathetically. Carried away by righteous indignity, Rashid seemed to have conveniently forgotten his own varied background; he'd been a pilot in the Pakistani air force, a professional cricketer, and a medical student before emigrating to England and becoming a successful restauranteur.

"Well, I suppose it's the economy," Powell ventured. "It must be hard for a small business to offer its employees much security these days."

Rashid's eyes flashed angrily. "If the bloody louts show up on time and do their bloody work without complaining, I will give them all the security they want and half their bloody tips besides."

Powell suppressed a smile only with some difficulty. "How will you manage?"

Rashid shrugged philosophically. "Nindi has agreed to come in when it gets busy, but I am hoping to have somebody new by next week. Now, enough of my small problems, how does it go with you?"

"Never a dull moment. Have I told you that Peter and David will be taking jobs in Canada this summer, working for Marion's brother in Vancouver? Peter's thinking of staying on and going to university there next year. David still has another year of school left and hasn't decided what he wants to do. They're all over there now on a reconnaissance mission, as a matter of fact. Marion was able to swing a conference in Vancouver, so she took the boys out of school for a couple of weeks."

Rashid nodded knowingly. "It is that time of life when the little birds are leaving the nest."

"Soon enough, I suppose," Powell said.

"And what about you and dear Marion? Have you decided what you will do when the time comes, my friend?"

"When the boys are gone? I don't know; travel a bit, perhaps. We haven't really talked about it."

"One cannot allow these things to happen haphazardly, my dear Erskine," Rashid said, a flicker of concern in his face. "Living one's life is like cooking a curry. One must have a plan of action. All the ingredients must be prepared beforehand, so as to be instantly available at precisely the moment when they are needed. The onions, garlic, and ginger must be browned just so, to prepare the foundation of the dish, then the spices added in the proper amounts and sequence. And finally the *masala* must be cooked *slowly*. The proper maturing of the flavors is the critical thing. You simply cannot rush it—to do so would be fatal to the intended result. And when the curry is ready, all will be in vain if the rice is not cooked to perfection and the *chapatis* are not piping hot. You yourself are a fine curry cook, Erskine, so you should know these things!" he concluded sternly.

Powell found the situation rather amusing. From anyone else such unsolicited, albeit cryptic, advice about his personal affairs would be highly unwelcome. However, Rashid seemed to know him better than he knew himself at times, and Powell had to admit that his friend had a point. All too often he put off important decisions until he was overtaken by events. He smiled and raised his glass. "Here's to planning."

Rashid beamed happily. "Now, then, I will go and personally prepare your dinner."

Powell demolished another *pappadam* and spent the next few minutes happily anticipating the gastronomic delights to come. Vegetable *samosas* to start: triangular pastries stuffed with mixed vegetables and lentils, deep-fried crisp and served with coconut chutney. And then the main course: *karai gosht*, tender pieces of lamb cooked quickly in an Indian wok with slivers of onions, fresh garlic and ginger, dried red chilies and green pepper; a side dish of *bhindi*: okra sauteed with onions and tomato, and flavored with cumin and coriander; basmati rice fragrant with aromatic spices and golden saffron; a small dish of spicy lime pickle; and last but not least a fluffy *naan* as big as an elephant's ear baked in the cylindrical clay tandoor. And then, to complete this veritable orgasm of the taste buds, a dessert created by Rashid in Powell's honor—Murder by Mango—a slab of mango ice cream splattered with raspberry *coulis*, the lot washed down with several cups of strong coffee. Then stagger home, burping richly. All things considered, Powell thought expansively, life didn't seem so bad from the cloistered perspective of the K2 Tandoori.

At nine-thirty the next morning Powell was at Paddington Station waiting for Detective-Sergeant Black to put in an appearance. He had arrived early and sat at a tiny coffee bar near the edge of the throng under the great curved roof of glass and wrought iron. The InterCity to Penzance, the train being rather ambitiously christened "The Cornish Riviera," didn't depart until ten thirty-five, and he was content to smoke and sip his coffee and watch the world pass by. The world that morning seemed to consist mostly of cheerful young women, casual in jumpers and skirts, with calf muscles knotting determinedly as they hurried to and from their trains. He tried to remember what it was like at that age, young hearts full of hope and tenderness. Little did they know. Not that he was completely immune to such romantic afflictions himself. It was rather like a glimpse through the rearview mirror of some half-forgotten landmark on the winding road that descends to the cemetery. He smiled faintly. It could be worse, he supposed.

He thought about the day last week when Marion and the boys left for Canada. A rare sunny morning of spring and she woke him early to make love. It had been like that lately, after not having done it for weeks. Never rains but it pours. It was always better between them afterward, and he wondered idly if sex wasn't a bit like electro-convulsive therapy. Soothes the savage breast. Grrr.

"I beg your pardon, sir?"

"Er, yes, miss. Another coffee, please, and, oh, yes, you'd better bring another cup. I'm expecting someone."

The waitress returned with the coffee, watching Powell from the side of her eye as she poured. They got all kinds in here, but not many like him. With his posh accent and just that hint of something in his eyes, she wondered if he was an artist of some sort, or perhaps an actor. Tall and dark with just a bit of gray to make him look distin-guished, like. Now that she thought about it, he did look a bit like Alan Bates. She wondered if he was expecting a man or a woman. A woman probably, someone cool and sexy—being something of a film buff, she pondered for a moment—someone like Sharon Stone. If she was dis-appointed a few minutes later when a stocky, balding man walked in and squeezed onto the stool beside Alan Bates, she gave no sign of it.

"Morning, Mr. Powell."

"Good morning, Bill. Raring to go?"

"It sounds interesting enough, sir."

"Oh, I don't know. A creature resembling the hound of the Baskervilles running amok in a quaint Cornish fish-ing village. Should be a piece of cake."

Black grinned. "How did we get pulled into it?"

Powell drew on his cigarette. "Evidently the local chief constable is under a bit of a cloud at the moment. Some-thing about unnatural couplings with farm animals."

Detective-Sergeant Black frowned disapprovingly.

"The superintendent in Camborne is an old chum of mine," Powell continued. "Things are rather in disarray out there, as you can imagine, and they are tending to view this Riddle of Penrick business as more of a distrac-tion than anything else. They've been taking a lot of flack from the press and are anxious to have the matter cleared up before the tourist season gets into full swing. One of the tabloids even had the cheek to suggest that the chief constable, being a dab hand with beasts, ought to take the case up himself. All things considered, they thought it best to bring in someone from outside, although it's not at all clear any crime's been committed."

Black grunted neutrally, seemingly lost in thought. Suddenly he brightened. *"A hound it was, an enormous coal-black hound, but not such a hound as mortal eyes have ever seen. Fire burst from its open mouth, its eyes glowed with a smouldering glare, its muzzle and hackles and dewlap were outlined in flickering flame."*

Powell looked up, startled. "What did you say?"

" 'The Hound of the Baskervilles,' sir."

Powell eyed his companion closely. "Very apt." Black was renowned at the Yard for his phenomenal memory, but impromptu literary quotations were rather out of character. Nonetheless, Powell was impressed.

Black looked pleased with himself.

Powell checked his watch. "Is that the time? We'd better take our seats."

Roger Trevenney stared out the window of his cottage. There was a red crabber off Towey Head, making for St. Ives like a spot of blood on the blue-green swell. A luminous mist had settled over the Head, whose dark shape seemed to float insubstantially between sea and sky in a hazy continuum of light. He had been sick again that morning and the headaches were getting worse, almost unbearable at times. He longed only to see the heavenly hosts praising the loving God and to be with Ruth and Millie at last. It wouldn't be long now, he knew. Only one more thing to do, the culmination of the lonely years, an eye for an eye, a tooth for a tooth, his holy mantra. And yet, as he neared the end there had been moments when his bitter resolve faltered, when the world around him seemed illuminated with a significance that he was only now beginning to grasp. When even the air itself was suffused with a pearly light, like a translucent curtain hanging between him and the final revelation. It had been the light that first inspired his modest efforts as a watercolorist, and while he needed to paint now more than ever to give life to his vision, his body had betrayed him.

Trevenney closed his eyes. He could see Ruth again, white spring frock dazzling in the sunlight, picking bluebells in the meadow above the sea cliffs. He remembered the picnic lunches by the secret tilted stones they had discovered together, blue sea below and yellow explosions of gorse all around them. He busy at his easel and Ruth writing in her diary.

Then he remembered the time she had been searching for shells on the sliver of beach below the cottage and found a *Clathrus*, its shell intricately carved into exquisite whorls and ridges, a larger, more colorful specimen than he had ever seen before. She had run up breathless to the cottage to show him, and then, fancying it a visitor from some tropical shore, had put it back into the sea. And the good-humored sparkle in her eyes when she had critiqued her father's paintings those many years ago. He wiped away a burning tear. God, how he missed her! So much like her mother and yet so different. The miracle of creation incarnate, her whole life ahead of her like a silver path of moonlight on the water . . . He slammed his fist down on the table.

Now it was starting all over again. He searched the window glass as if it were a mirror. The mist had thick-ened, obscuring Towey Head from view. He cradled his head in his hands and wept soundlessly.

CHAPTER 2

Detective-Sergeant Black turned right off the B3300 just before Portreath onto the minor road that led to Penrick and to Porthtowan beyond. Powell interrupted his travelogue momentarily to lower the passenger-side window. He took a deep breath. The air was bracing with the faint but unmistakable astringency of the sea. He lit a cigarette. The road undulated over scrubby fields punctuated by occasional roofless engine houses with crumbling chimneys, abandoned mines with names like Wheal Faith and Wheal Bounty. Stark reminders of the Duchy's past riches.

"It's amazing to think that Bronze Age men were streaming and smelting tin here three thousand years ago," Powell remarked.

Black grunted with apparent interest. "You seem to know a lot about Cornwall, sir."

"During my annual summer pilgrimages to Bude with Marion and the boys I've found ample opportunity to dabble in the local history. I'm not much of a beach person, I'd rather be poking around some old ruins."

"I'm the same way, sir."

"By the way, what did you think of our session with the locals yesterday?" After arriving in Camborne they'd spent the previous afternoon being briefed by the local superintendent.

"Well, sir, I get the impression they're not exactly thrilled about our being here."

Powell smiled. "Superintendent Harrison and I go back a long way. It's only natural to protect one's turf, of course, but I suspect he's secretly relieved to get the file off his desk. And he was good enough to loan us a car."

"They seem to think it's a fairly routine job."

"Perhaps. But I have a hunch there may be more to it than meets the eye; I'm hoping that Chief Inspector Butts in St. Ives will be able to fill in some of the blanks. All, no doubt, will be revealed in the fullness of time."

The road began to rise slightly, then dipped abruptly into the grassy valley of the River Teal.

"Wasn't it Chesterton who wrote that the rolling English road was made by the rolling English drunk?" Black observed casually.

"Something like that." Once again Powell was taken aback. It seemed there was indeed another side to his old colleague that he had hitherto not recognized.

As they descended, the valley gradually narrowed to a steep ravine with small white and cream houses clinging to its sides above a burbling stream, the roadside ditches alight with yellow primroses. After a few hundred yards the valley opened up again to reveal a fetching prospect, a fine stone church with the sparkling blue sea as a backdrop. Having delved into his collection of travel guides before leaving home, Powell knew that the church had been built in the fourteenth century and dedicated to St. Penrick, who had arrived at the estuary of the River Teal in a coracle from Ireland in the sixth century. His was a grimly ascetic order who, amongst their many rituals of spiritual purification, would stand immersed to their necks in ice-cold water amidst the granite megaliths erected by the ancestors of their newfound congregation, reciting psalters and praying for the conversion of the heathen. Powell supposed that the current vicar, in his own way, still labored in the same fields.

"Pull over here," he directed.

The churchyard afforded a fine view of the village below and the surrounding stretch of coastline. A stone bridge crossed the stream at the foot of the steep hill below the church. A mile-long arc of tawny sand confined by two steep promontories—the larger, Towey Head, to the southwest—encircling the bay like two claws. The narrow river channel marked by straggling poles, a few brightly painted fishing boats propped up on the sand waiting for high tide, and color-washed cottages piled tier upon tier up the hillside, with the church set like a beacon on top. A spiritual lighthouse for the lost souls of Penrick.

"Lovely," remarked Detective-Sergeant Black, who was not usually given to such outbursts.

Powell could only assume that his companion was at a loss for a suitable quotation, so he stepped into the breach:

"Thy shores are empires, changed in all save thee;
Assyria, Greece, Rome, Carthage, what are they?
Thy waters wasted them while they were free . . ."

Without missing a beat, Black continued solemnly:

"Unchangeable save to the wild waves' play,
Time writes no wrinkles on thine azure brow;
Such as creation's dawn beheld, thou rollest now."

Then he smiled equably. "I quite like Lord Byron."

Any lingering suspicion that Sergeant Black was a mere literary dilettante was dispelled once and for all. Powell's casual serve had been expertly returned; he realized he would have to place his shots more carefully in the future. "We'd better get settled in," he said. "I understand our accommodation comes highly commended by Butts."

Amongst the cottages ran a maze of streets and alleys barely wide enough for a car, but Black eventually negotiated a route down to the water's edge. Powell experienced a sinking feeling as a closer inspection revealed that the village center consisted of a few unremarkable shops and guesthouses clustered around the tiny harbor. More promising was a plain but elegant Georgian pub, the Head, which was painted, appropriately enough, pink. There were a few people strolling along the front, taking the morning air.

They soon located the Wrecker's Rest Guesthouse, the premises of George and Agnes Polfrock, straight out of Fawlty bloody Towers, as Detective-Sergeant Black was later to remark in the Head over a pint. The best thing that could be said for the Wrecker's Rest was that it had come recommended by Chief Inspector Butts, but this turned out to be a dubious distinction indeed. Powell had to admit that its whitewashed facade with flower boxes and mullioned windows looking out over the quay, cluttered with lobster traps and crab pots, the sweep of yellow sand and the wide blue Atlantic beyond, possessed a certain superficial charm—*picturesque chic* was the expression that came to mind. However this notion was quickly dispelled by the pervasive aura of the proprietors, which permeated the premises like a pungent odor.

"Ooo, Chief Superintendent Powell! It isn't often we have guests from Scotland Yard," Mrs. Polfrock gushed. She was a squarish, lumpy woman with improbable red hair. "And this must be . . ."

"Detective-Sergeant Black, madam," Black volunteered.

"Yes, of course. We've prepared the Smuggler's Suite for you, Chief Superintendent, commanding a fine view of the Sands and Towey Head. And Sergeant, er, I'm sorry . . ."

"Black, madam," Black prompted between clenched teeth.

"Yes, of course. We've put you in the back. Now if you'll just sign the guest registry I'll have my husband, George, show you to your rooms. Buttie didn't say how long you would be staying," she added, as if by way of casual chitchat.

Powell cocked an eyebrow. "Buttie?"

"Alf Butts, my brother-in-law."

"*Chief Inspector* Butts, oh I see!" Powell was beginning to wonder if their being maneuvered to the Wrecker's Rest was simple nepotism or Buttie putting the boot in for being muscled off his turf.

Mrs. Polfrock clucked disapprovingly. "All this publicity is bad for business, although I don't believe a word of it myself, and even Buttie says it's a load of codswallop. Don't you agree, Chief Superintendent?"

"That's what we're here to find out, Mrs. Polfrock."

She smiled fixedly, her mouth a thick red smudge of lipstick. Then without warning she let out a bellow. "George!"

Powell swore he could feel the roof slates rattle.

George Polfrock came scurrying, a little man much smaller than his wife, balding, with nervous, darting eyes. "Yes, my sweet," he panted, catching his breath and sizing up his new guests. He reminded one of a Pekingese, eager for a treat.

"Show Chief Superintendent Powell and, er, the sergeant to their rooms." It was clearly an order, not a request. "By the way, will you gentlemen be taking lunch?"

"I think not, Mrs. Polfrock. Thanks all the same. We had a late breakfast in Camborne and we're anxious to get started."

Her eyes narrowed suspiciously. "As you like, but please remember that I require at least four hours' notice to reserve a place for lunch and the evening meal."

"We'll bear that in mind, Mrs. Polfrock. Do you get many guests this time of year?" Powell inquired innocently.

A grudging shrug. "Besides you two, there's just that *person* from the press." She looked as if she had just swallowed something nasty. "But in a month's time we'll be full up right through the season."

Powell picked up his suitcase. "Splendid. Lead the way, Mr. Polfrock."

Fifteen minutes later Powell and Black fled the Wrecker's Rest and made a beeline for the pub.

* * *

"Bloody charming," Black said as he tucked into his fish and chips.

They had the place to themselves and Powell, having reluctantly eschewed a selection from the surprisingly extensive wine list, savored his first pint of Cornish bitter since the previous summer. He smacked his lips appreciatively. "Ah, well, I trust we won't be spending too many cozy evenings with our hosts gathered together around the hearth." He poked at his ploughman's. "Still, Butts has got a nerve, don't you think? Although he probably didn't have much choice, considering—"

He was interrupted by the publican, who had come over to introduce himself. Tall and wide and beginning to bulge in the wrong places, the man looked like a rugby player gone to seed.

"Tony Rowlands at your service," he said heartily. "Is everything all right?"

"Excellent, thank you." Powell introduced Black and himself. "Very nice place you have here." Always wise to open with a platitude.

Rowlands smiled. "We try to add a little class to the neighborhood. I've lived here for over thirty years and I'm still working at it." He pulled up a chair and sat down. "Just passing through?"

"We're staying at the Wrecker's Rest for a few days."

Rowlands smirked. "There's an odd couple if ever there was one. She's a horrible old shrew and he's a raving pervert. Spies on the young girls at Mawgawan Beach with a telescope."

Powell wasn't quite sure whether he found this display of candor refreshing or slightly off-putting. More the former, he decided, as it confirmed his own first impression of the Polfrocks.

"What brings you gentlemen to Penrick—business or pleasure?" Rowlands inquired easily.

Powell explained that they were policemen and had come to investigate the so-called Riddle.

Rowlands was suddenly tight-lipped.

"Mrs. Polfrock says it's bad for business," Powell ventured.

"That depends on how you look at it. After all, I've just got two new customers, haven't I?"

Powell raised his glass. "Soon to be regulars, I think."

"Well, you've come to the right place, Chief Superintendent," a feminine voice piped in. The sturdy blonde barmaid, who looked like she was genetically predisposed to pull pints, came over to their table. "I couldn't help overhearing that you gentlemen are from Scotland Yard, here to investigate the sightings. I was the first to see it, wasn't I, love?"

Rowlands rolled his eyes but said nothing.

Powell reached over and pulled a chair out from the table. "Please sit down, Miss, er . . . ?"

"Thompson. But you can call me Jenny."

"Right then, Jenny, why don't you tell us all about it?"

"It was a week ago last Monday after closing time— two weeks ago today that would be," she began breathlessly. "I went for a walk along the Sands, down toward the Head. The tide was in, so there was just that narrow strip of beach to walk along. I was just coming around a small point of rock when I saw a faint light at the water's edge, sort of a greenish glow. I wondered what it was, so I went a little closer. Well, I nearly fainted on the spot! It was someone or some *thing* trying to crawl out of the water. It was all furry and wrinkled, with a strange halo all around and"—she shuddered—"it didn't have a head!"

Detective-Sergeant Black cleared his throat politely.

Powell ignored him. "Are you sure, Miss, er, Jenny?"

She nodded earnestly. "I know she didn't! I swear to God, her neck just sort of ended and—"

"You said *she*," Powell interjected.

Jenny seemed slightly taken aback, as if it had just struck her for the first time. "I don't know why, exactly, but I'm sure it was a she."

"You said it was trying to crawl out of the water," Powell said gravely. "Are you certain it was moving of its own accord?"

She looked indignant. "I wasn't about to stick around to find out, was I?"

"No, I suppose not. What did you do next?"

"I ran back here as fast as I could to tell Tone. Didn't I, Tone?"

"That's right," Rowlands said. "The poor girl looked like death warmed over—"

"Tony!" Jenny admonished.

He smiled. "Sorry, love, figure of speech. Anyway, I grabbed a torch and my twelve bore and went back to look for it. I'm pretty sure I found the right spot, but I'm damned if I could find anything. At the time I thought that Jen was seeing things, but the next night it was spotted again by somebody else. Isn't that right, love?" He gave her a sharp slap on the bottom.

A gesture of familiarity or admonishment? Powell wondered.

Jenny looked none too pleased. "That's right, Tone."

Rowlands shrugged. "That's the goods. It's been seen on the Sands several times since, between here and the Head, always at night."

"What do you make of it?" Powell asked.

Rowlands regarded Powell shrewdly before replying. "The damn thing gives me the creeps, if you want to know the truth, but I think it's pretty obvious, don't you?"

"Go on."

"It's something drifting in and out with the tide. It turns up here and it turns up there."

"Yes, but what?"

Rowlands shifted uneasily in his chair. "You tell me."

The surf crashed riotously against the rocks and Nick Tebble pulled smartly, expertly timing his strokes so that the tiny skiff rode the swells as smoothly as any Malibu surfer. Gulls clamored overhead, wheeling and plunging as if harrying a school of herring. He stayed his oars momentarily. "Bugger off, yer greedy bastards," he shouted above the din.

The birds took no notice so he began to row again, straining at the oars now and making for a small cove, perhaps fifty feet wide and twice as deep, that had suddenly opened up in the looming cliff face. A dozen more pulls and the skiff was deposited abruptly on a patch of shingled beach in front of a gray stone house that looked like it had grown organically from the surrounding rock. Above the door, carved in the granite lintel, were the words THE OLD FISH CELLAR and, underneath, *DULCIS*

LUCRI ODOR. A lane behind the house climbed steeply to the turf-covered heights above.

He clambered out and dragged the boat a few feet farther up the beach. Trailing the bow rope behind him like an umbilical cord, he trudged toward the house. The shingle gave way to shelving rock slabs up to the base of a stone wall taller than a man, encrusted with barnacles and stained black with lichens above the tide line. The wall was surmounted by a narrow set of steps. He tied the line to a rusted iron ring set into the wall and then looked back down the beach with squinting eyes. There was one more thing he had to do, but it could wait until he'd had a drink.

Hadn't his grandfather been a fisherman in these waters during the heyday, and his young father a *huer*, directing the boats from the clifftops to the vast shoals of pilchards that had once filled all the bays and coves along the Cornish coast? *"Heva! Heva!"* they'd cry when the fish were spotted, then the boats would encircle the schools with their seines—countless thousands of them flashing silver like precious coins. On a good day they'd haul in a million or more. Then one year, mysteriously, the pilchards vanished, never to return again. Caught by the Frenchies, Tebble reckoned. Nothing left but a few mackerel and sharks for the tourists to catch and the ghosts of once bustling harbors up and down the coast.

And what about the foreigners that had knacked the mines when the ore ran out with never a thought for Cousin Jack? Now they returned by the thousands every summer like vermin, plugging up the lanes so you couldn't move in the village. (Just last year, one of them had got his car wedged tight in Plover Street, demolishing old Mrs. Vivian's flower boxes and launching her geraniums like red rockets into the street.) They threw their money around as if to mock every Cornishman who'd ever tried to make an honest living in the earth or on the sea. And the only ones to profit by it were the scum that lived off them.

He drew himself up. But wasn't he a fair-trader, just like them that had gone before him? He spat and grinned slyly. And he had all the time in the world. Or so he thought. Hunched and careful, he made his way up the slime-coated steps.

CHAPTER 3

The needles of water made her skin tingle. She ran her hands lightly over her breasts and felt the nipples harden. Marvelous little items, she thought; brilliantly utilitarian, exquisitely responsive to both physical and emotional stimuli—not to mention air conditioners—and the latest preoccupation of the fashion world. One went to considerable lengths, it seemed, to deal with erect nipples, either to conceal them or to flaunt them, as the case might be. The last word on the subject was undoubtedly the recent declaration in the *Sunday Times* that it's no longer considered rude to point. Although she didn't feel strongly about it one way or the other, she was prepared to stand up and be counted (she had, after all, no particular interest in discounting potential assets).

She looked down at the curve of her belly and frowned. Not as flat as it used to be; still, she was thirty-five and had held up pretty well, all things considered. Physical appearance had never been that important to her, but then she supposed she was more fortunate than most in that department. In the end it didn't seem to matter much; she hadn't exactly been lucky in love, and these days she could hardly be bothered.

But all in all, she was basically content with her life. A small inheritance from her father provided her with almost enough to live on, and she had her writing to sustain her intellectually and creatively, if not yet financially. There were times when she wondered if that rose-covered cottage she longed for wouldn't get a bit lonely during the long winter nights, but she tried not to feel too sorry for herself. She had made certain choices and was prepared to live with them. And besides, she still had a few good innings left.

She located a minute sliver of soap and began to lather herself vigorously. Suddenly she let out a piercing shriek. "Bloody hell!" In an instant the shower spray had turned from tepid to ice-cold. Swearing creatively between clenched teeth, she fumbled with the knob and eventually managed to staunch the glacial flow. Out of all the guesthouses in Cornwall, how in heaven's name had she ever picked this one? She had been seeking a quiet, seaside setting to get the creative juices flowing, not a bout of pneumonia!

She squeezed out of the shower stall and wrapped herself in the undersized towel that had been provided. A few spring weeks in Cornwall before the hordes of holidaymakers descended, to work on her book—a sort of romantic comedy about a thirtysomething professional couple who chuck sophisticated London for a life of self-sufficiency on the Cornish coast. It had seemed like a good idea at the time. She'd be free to get up when she wished, write when she felt like it, and generally soak up the atmosphere that was so important to her as a writer.

Her first novel had been published the previous year to some modest acclaim, and she was now under considerable pressure from her publisher to produce another. But after the first blush of success had faded, the enormity of the task had proven daunting. In fact, there were moments when she wasn't sure she had another book in her. Looking back, it seemed as if the first one had written itself, perhaps because she had thought about it for so long, to the point where she had basically composed the entire story in her head before sitting down at the keyboard. Even though it had taken nearly three years to finish, working in fits and starts with the usual frustrations and rejection slips, all she could remember was the heady rush of creativity that had characterized that period in her life. Now she was working to a deadline, which was quite a different matter. Her worst fear was that she'd exhausted her store of ideas, used up all the clever turns of phrase and erudite allusions that she'd assiduously filed away over the years. She finally concluded that the only thing for it, if she wasn't to bog down completely, was a stint in Cornwall to steep herself in the setting of her new book.

So here she was in Penrick on the north coast of Cornwall, a spectacular spot with a romantic history of shipwrecks and smuggling and plenty of atmosphere à la Daphne du Maurier. It was just as she had imagined it. There was a catch, of course, as there always is. But in this instance it turned out to be a rather large one: the Polfrocks. The perils of Agnes the Dragon Lady were obvious and fairly easily countered, but the husband, George, who appeared to play a secondary role at the Wrecker's Rest (but apparently not, in the absence of any evidence of little Polfrocks, a procreative one), was more of a problem. His chief hobby seemed to be creeping about and mentally undressing any woman—save his wife, one presumed—who came within a hundred yards. Jane had to continually suppress the paranoid notion that Georgie Boy was accustomed to having it off behind peepholes in the rooms of his female guests.

But there had been trade-offs. Almost unbelievably, she had met a couple in the pub who had dropped out of the rat race a few years ago to make their living growing flowers up near Towey Head! They had provided a well of useful information for her book. And she had been in the right place at the right time to capitalize on the Riddle of Penrick, as she had so described the mysterious apparition on the Penrick Sands in her debut as a journalist.

While reading English literature at university she had taken a course in journalism, spending a summer working for one of the London tabloids as a sort of general dogsbody. The experience had proven memorable in more ways than one. She had made a number of contacts at the newspaper, some of which she had maintained. One in particular had been romantic—and an unmitigated disaster, as it turned out. She still occasionally bumped into the bloke, who was now a senior editor at one of the larger London dailies.

When the Riddle was first sighted a few days after she had ensconced herself at the Wrecker's Rest, she called Michael to tip him off to a possible story. He had been preoccupied with some Royal hijinks at the time and suggested that she take a stab at writing the story herself. If she agreed to file an exclusive report with his paper, he had promised to recycle any subsequent installments for the wire services on her behalf, under her own byline, assuming of course that the story turned out to be more than just a one-day wonder. For old times' sake, as he had put it. Fancying herself quite the starving artist, she had swallowed her pride and leapt at the chance to make a few quid. It would get her mind off the novel, and at least she would be writing.

As a news item, the Riddle had so far remained a minor curiosity relegated to the back pages, but even so, she had managed to sell a few lines. A reporter from the local paper in St. Ives had put in a brief appearance but soon lost interest, so she more or less had the field to herself. It was almost certainly a hoax of some kind (which she was determined to get to the bottom of) but a fortuitous and welcome diversion nonetheless. And one never knew, she might be onto something that would eventually rival the Beast of Bodmin Moor in notoriety. Jane Goode, freelance journalist, informing the curious masses. It seemed rather romantic, and it was all grist for the mill. Perhaps she could work the idea into her novel somehow.

She pulled on a pair of jeans and then selected a particularly shapeless jersey to frustrate Mr. Polfrock. She smiled grimly. She was looking forward to having a word with the Dragon Lady about the so-called amenities of the Wrecker's Rest. *All mod cons,* like hell!

After lunch Powell set out along the Sands toward Towey Head, leaving Sergeant Black behind to explore Penrick. He strolled along the beach, familiarizing himself with the territory and mulling over his initial suspicions about the strange sightings on the Penrick Sands. He had already concluded that there was something decidedly fishy about the entire business.

The tide was well out and the sky was a hazy gray dome speckled with screaming gulls. A gusty wind was whipping up white horses on the blue curve of sea, which sat like a meniscus atop a yellow band of sand. What nautical instincts he retained from his university sailing days told him a change of weather was in the offing. A few hardy souls were on the beach, clinging to deck chairs or huddled behind colorful nylon windbreaks that flapped wildly like kites straining to take off.

To his left was an area of wasteland, the towans, a mixture of sand and sea rush heaped high by the wind into a chaotic jumble of dunes. The effect was a bit eerie, a half-mile wall of sand, up to twenty feet high and several hundred yards wide, that effectively isolated the beach from the base of the low cliffs beyond. In the distant past, hurricanes of sand had inundated stretches of the northern Cornish coast, and in places whole farmsteads (and even a lost city, it is purported) had been overwhelmed and now lie buried, preserved like villas in Pompeii. One could only marvel at the caprice of nature.

"Look on my works, ye Mighty, and despair!"
Nothing beside remains. Round the decay
Of that colossal wreck, boundless and bare
The lone and level sands stretch far away.

Powell smiled thinly. Sergeant Black would no doubt appreciate Shelley's sentiment.

The Sands gradually petered out and the beach became

rockier in character where the cliffs pinched in toward the sea before soaring to the summit of Towey Head. Beneath the promontory, a seashore clutter of bungalows lined the little cove that formed the southwest corner of Penrick Bay. Most were still boarded up for the season.

An elderly man pottered about with an outboard engine near a small shed beside one of the cottages. It was better kept than its neighbors—its fenced-off garden bright with sea pinks and lavender.

He had gray hair slicked back and bushy eyebrows. In his early seventies, Powell guessed. "Good afternoon," he called out.

The man looked up from his work, then wiped his hands on a greasy rag. He eyed Powell's tweed jacket critically. "It's going to rain, you know," he rejoined sternly.

"Ah, well, I'm not easily deterred."

"I suppose you're another one of those newspaper people."

"Good heavens, no!" Powell looked genuinely shocked. Then he smiled. "It's worse than that, actually."

The man looked irritated. "I beg your pardon?"

"I'm a policeman."

At first the man looked surprised, then he nodded knowingly. "Oh, I see! I was wondering when you'd show up. The name's Harris."

Powell, slightly puzzled, introduced himself. "You weren't expecting me by any chance, were you, Mr. Harris?"

"Well, not you *personally*, Chief Superintendent, but somebody *like* you. And it's *Dr.* Harris, by the way. Come inside the house so we can chat."

Mildly intrigued, Powell turned to follow his host into the cottage, and as he did so something caught his attention. Someone was standing in the small front window of the cottage next door, but as he turned his head to get a better look, the figure moved away, merging into the shadows.

Dr. Harris's tiny sitting room, cluttered with books and papers, had a distinctly nautical flavor: a tarnished brass telescope mounted on a tripod at the front window, and on the adjoining wall a Victorian barometer, a ship's clock, and several framed photographs of a sleek ketch— the *Dulcinea*—crewed by a young man (a younger Dr. Harris?) and a smiling woman. At Harris's invitation he took a seat on a threadbare settee.

Powell stared at the wall behind Dr. Harris, transfixed. In a small alcove to the right of, and not visible from, the doorway hung a stunning painting of a familiar scene. "Do you mind?" he asked.

Harris smiled. "Be my guest."

Powell got up and went over to examine the painting. It was a watercolor, approximately two-and-a-half by three feet in size and simply breathtaking in its conception and execution. The artist had employed the brilliant transparency of light and the shifting fluidity of water to permeate and absorb the merest suggestion of solid shapes, which hardly seemed to be seen at all. Sea-swept cliffs, a colorful splash of cottages, and in the foreground a yacht, the whole overshadowed by the looming presence of Towey Head. The perspective seemed slightly odd, as if the artist had set out to show the space between objects as a greater or lesser concentration of light rather than simply as physical distance. "It's bloody marvelous!" he said.

"Yes it is, rather," Harris said quietly.

"I can't make out the signature."

"Roger Trevenney. He lives near here, past Mawgawan Beach."

"For a moment there I thought you'd lifted a Turner from the Tate Gallery."

"I'd rather have Roger's painting, to tell the truth. Surprisingly, he's not that well known, but he's a genius nonetheless. He lost his daughter tragically some years ago and hasn't done much since. Paints for friends, mostly, and sells the odd one to make ends meet."

"You know him, then?"

"Yes."

"That must be the *Dulcinea* in the painting."

"You're very observant, Chief Superintendent."

"She looks a most excellent mistress."

"Bravo! You don't sail by any chance?"

"Not anymore, I'm afraid."

Harris nodded sadly. "A quick turn around the bay in my little Enterprise now and again, that's about my speed these days."

"I'd very much like to meet him."

Harris stiffened slightly. "I beg your pardon?"

"Trevenney."

Harris frowned. "He's not very well—he really shouldn't be disturbed."

That seemed to be that. "I see."

Harris rubbed his hands together briskly. "Now, then, a little restorative is what the doctor ordered. Glass of wine?"

Powell smiled. "I would never argue with a medical man."

Harris returned with two glasses of white wine. "I've a fondness for Burgundy, and 'ninety-five was an excellent year."

After the obligatory rituals, Powell took a lingering sip. He was impressed. "Very nice."

Harris looked pleased. "There's more where that came from, Chief Superintendent." He winked slyly.

Thus lubricated, Dr. Harris began to recount his life story. After qualifying in London some forty years ago, he had no idea where he wanted to settle down and practice. He came out to Cornwall for a holiday—to sow his wild oats, as he put it—where he met a young student working at a hotel in St. Ives for the summer (Helen Morrison, Powell learned, the smiling woman in the photographs). They found they had much in common—an affinity for the sea and sailing, in particular—and soon fell madly in love. Upon returning to London, they married, she finished her degree in fine arts, and Harris worked for a time as a resident at St. Bart's. They very quickly discovered, however, that life in the city was not for them. Throwing caution to the wind, they pulled up roots and followed their hearts back to St. Ives. He set up a family practice, and she opened a small art shop. That was how they had met Trevenney, Harris added as an aside. They acquired the *Dulcinea* and spent their summers sailing up and down the Cornish coast. The years passed happily.

"It was an idyllic sort of existence, looking back on it. We were deeply in love, living the life we'd chosen in the most beautiful spot on earth. I suppose deep down one realized that it couldn't go on forever, but one is never really prepared for the end." He paused. "Helen was killed in a car crash in nineteen-eighty."

"I'm sorry," Powell murmured.

"Ah, well, Chief Superintendent, the grim reaper is no stranger to either of us. Now, a bit more wine, I think."

After Harris had returned with their glasses replenished, he continued, "I sold everything about ten years ago, the *Dulcinea*, my practice, and leased this place. It's quite nice, really. Penrick is fairly quiet most of the year. It gets a bit hectic during the summer months, but nothing like St. Ives or Perranporth. It's a pleasant enough life; I do a bit of gardening to pass the time . . ." He suddenly looked very tired.

Powell cleared his throat. "Sir, you said before that you'd been expecting someone like me to call. What did you mean, exactly?"

Harris was suddenly angry. "It's about bloody time someone put a stop to it! Whoever is responsible for this—this abomination—should be put away for a very long time! Do you know how much suffering it's caused already?"

"I'm sorry, I'm not sure that I understand . . ."

Harris looked embarrassed. "Please forgive me, Chief Superintendent, it's—it's just that it simply cannot be allowed to continue. I mean, I'm pleased that the police have finally been brought in, that's all. I assume that's why you are here."

"You're referring to the so-called Riddle of Penrick, I take it?"

Harris nodded wearily.

Powell examined his host closely, without appearing to do so. "Have you seen it yourself?"

Harris seemed slightly offended by the question. "No, of course not. It's obviously a load of rubbish, a malicious prank of some kind."

"But you said that someone has suffered as a result of it . . ."

Harris shrugged unconvincingly. "Well, you know, reporters snooping around, the invasion of one's privacy, and now the police."

Powell was disappointed. "I see. You're a man of science, Dr. Harris; assuming you're right about the Riddle, do you have any idea what it might be?"

Harris hesitated before replying. "I reckon it's an animal carcass of some kind, done up to look human and then dragged onto the beach at night."

Powell was doubtful. "But why would anyone go to so much trouble?"

Harris fixed him with a penetrating gaze. "That's the question, isn't it?"

Powell fired a shot in the dark. "Is there anyone you can think of who might be able to point me in the right direction?"

Harris seemed to consider the question carefully. "There are basically two kinds of people in Penrick, Chief Superintendent: locals and outsiders. And two subclasses of outsiders, come to that—those like myself and the young couple next door, for instance, who have chosen to live here; and the mobs of holidaymakers who swarm into our fair village each summer. Putting it diplomatically, one could say that the locals have an ambivalent attitude toward tourists, who are, sad to say, the mainstay of the local economy these days, and a major source of aggravation. A seasonal stampede of cash cows might be the best way to describe it. I like to think we permanent transplants are generally better tolerated. To answer your question: No, I don't think I can enlighten you further, but you should at least be aware that there are various interests to consider."

An intriguing and somewhat ambiguous answer that nonetheless skirted the main issue: Who stood to gain by the Riddle? Powell drained his glass. "I won't take up any more of your time, Dr. Harris. I'm grateful for your hospitality."

"Don't mention it. Pop in anytime. I'd welcome the company," he added a bit wistfully. "The pub has a decent cellar, by the way."

Powell smiled. "I'll keep it in mind."

On a whim, Powell walked over to the neighboring cottage, picking his way through the cluttered yard, and knocked on the door. There was no answer. As he walked back along the Sands toward the village, immersed in his thoughts, he noticed that a damp mist had rolled in from the sea. Dr. Harris had aroused his curiosity; he was a likable chap, but he had responded in a very personal way when the subject of the Riddle had come up and then tried to gloss over his reaction. Who was suffering? And what exactly was the cause of it? Surely not some elaborate hoax—that became increasingly implausible the more he thought about it. Whistling tunelessly, he had no doubt that he would be seeing Dr. Harris again.

CHAPTER 4

A sudden fierce squall raged outside. The rain, driven by gusts of wind, rattled like handfuls of gravel tossed against the windowpane. Powell and Black sat bleakly in the Residents' Lounge of the Wrecker's Rest while Mrs. Polfrock held forth on a dizzying variety of subjects, relentlessly plumbing the depths of banality and narrow-mindedness for the benefit of what was, for all intents and purposes, a captive audience.

After enduring a dinner that consisted of underdone lamb chops anointed with a substance resembling motor oil, accompanied by soggy chips and tinned sweet corn (the vegetable *du jour*, according to the menu), Powell and Black had been on their way out to the pub to lick their wounds when they were cornered by Mrs. Polfrock, who had herded them as expertly as any sheepdog into the Residents' Lounge. She liked to mingle with the guests, was the way she put it, which is to say she liked to pry as obtrusively as possible into their personal affairs.

Powell's spirits were sinking rapidly like a piece of

Cornish granite dropped into the Atlantic Ocean. Things were not turning out exactly the way he had planned. His initial reaction at being offered the assignment in Cornwall had been one of guarded enthusiasm. Something a bit out of the ordinary: curious happenings on the Cornish coast, himself ensconced for the duration in some picturesque seaside hotel, with Keith Floyd presiding over the kitchen, wineglass in hand, burbling happily about fresh English ingredients lovingly prepared. More to the point, he had badly needed a break from the usual day-to-day drudgery and domestic turmoil. He had already decided with considerable reluctance to forgo his annual salmon fishing holiday in Scotland with his old Scottish mate and colleague, Alex Barrett. The last time around they had become embroiled in a messy murder investigation, the personal implications of which Powell was still trying to sort through. He and Barrett were planning to get together in September for a bit of rough shooting, but September seemed a long way off.

Not that he hadn't had some reservations about taking the case. First off, there was the possibility, indeed the high probability that the Riddle of Penrick would turn out to have a perfectly mundane explanation, the end result being that he would have squandered a precious Murder Squad assignment. More ominous was the fact that Sir Henry Merriman, Assistant Commissioner of the Metropolitan Police, had offered it to him in the first place. Powell was convinced—irrationally, he knew—that Merriman had it in for him. Sir Henry was a ruthlessly ambitious and calculating sycophant, which tended to compensate, careerwise at least, for his considerable shortcomings. His latest fixation was the planning of a multimillion-pound police theme park and museum in central London called The Police Experience ("a day of chills, mystery, and suspense for the whole family"). This at least had the advantage of diverting his attention away from legitimate policing issues where he could do some real damage.

Powell was the very antithesis of Merriman. Throughout his career he had been promoted, not through any particular desire on his part to climb the bureaucratic stairway to heaven, but by virtue of an intuitive bent that bordered on brilliance and an ability to get the job done, even if his methods were somewhat informal at times. His talents had been recognized early by his superiors, but not always by himself.

In the end, his desire for a change of scene had won out, and thus it was he found himself in the Residents' Lounge of the Wrecker's Rest being subjected to the tedious pontificating of Mrs. Agnes Polfrock.

"It's them students at Mawgawan Beach and them others besides," she was saying, "running around in the altogether, having orgies and I don't know what else. It's disgusting."

Powell tried in vain to picture in his mind what the *what else* could be.

And Mr. Polfrock, imagining perhaps the curtailment of his frequent birding expeditions with his spotting scope to the cliffs overlooking Mawgawan Beach, muttered, "What bloody rubbish!"

"I couldn't agree more, Mrs. Polfrock," Powell remarked breezily. "One must maintain certain standards. I'll have a word with Chief Inspector Butts. The local constabulary will no doubt wish to keep, er, abreast of such activities." Good Christ, how was he going to put up with any more of her drivel? He belched silently. He held Sergeant Black, whom he had instructed to gather sufficient culinary intelligence in and around Penrick so they could avoid any such unpleasant surprises, and who now refused to meet his eye, personally responsible.

Mrs. Polfrock nodded smugly. "Do have another piece of gâteau, Chief Superintendent."

"Nice bit of cake, that," opined Mr. Polfrock.

"Married are you, Mr. Powell?" Mrs Polfrock inquired out of the blue.

Before Powell could formulate an appropriate reply, he heard the front door slam and a few seconds later a woman, cloaked in a purdah of dripping oilskins, burst into the room.

"I've bloody seen it!" she cried. She seemed more excited than upset about it, whatever *it* was.

"What is it, woman?" Mrs. Polfrock snapped irritably.

"On the beach, down along the towans!" the woman replied breathlessly. "The Riddle of Penrick. I've solved it, but—wouldn't you know it?— I left my damn camera behind!" She stood in the middle of the room blinking incredulously at her audience. "How can you just sit there—doesn't anyone want to see it?"

Powell rose to his feet and introduced himself and Sergeant Black. "I for one am champing at the bit. Lead the way, Ms., er . . . ?"

"Goode. Jane Goode." She pulled off her hood, loosing a flood of auburn hair. She smiled sweetly. "Nice to meet you, Mr. Powell. I'm always happy to assist the police."

Powell looked her over with considerable interest. "As they say, Ms. Goode, the proof is in the pudding."

"Truer words were never spoken, Chief Superintendent."
He cleared his throat. "After you, then."

"I'll just get my camera. I'll meet you in the front hall
in two minutes."

"Right." Powell turned to Black with that chilling
smile the sergeant knew all too well. "You stay here and
keep Mr. and Mrs. Polfrock company. It's a filthy night;
there's no point in both of us catching our death."

Powell, feeling rather pleased with himself, headed up
to his room to fetch his rain gear. As he climbed the
stairs, he heard Mrs. Polfrock remark (somewhat incon-
gruously, it seemed to him under the circumstances),
"Look here, George, the bloody bitch has left a wet spot
on the rug."

Between Land's End and the east coast of Newfound-
land there lies about three thousand miles of open ocean,
enabling an ambitious late-season Atlantic storm, like the
one that prevailed that evening, to take a serious run at
the north coast of Cornwall. It occurred to Powell as he
leaned into the gale, squinting against a driving mixture
of rain and sand and trying to keep to the narrow beach
path illuminated faintly in his torch beam, that the
sudden appearance of Jane Goode had brightened considerably his dreary evening. He shone his torch momentarily at her back, which was on the verge of disappearing
from view as she hurried ahead. He wondered idly what
she looked like underneath her Barbour. The tide was
well in, and big rollers were breaking on the beach.
Rivulets of cold water streamed down his face. He ran
the tip of his tongue over his upper lip and tasted the
saltspray. Amidst the tumult of wind and rain, he could

hear the boom of the surf pounding against the rocks of Towey Head. Except for the glow of his torch beam and the occasional flicker of light up ahead that marked his companion's progress, he felt utterly alone with the elements. After his evening with the Polfrocks, the sensation was not entirely unpleasant.

Jane Goode stopped to wait for Powell. She shivered convulsively. It didn't take much to imagine that she was back in her drafty room at the Wrecker's Rest taking a shower. She jumped when she felt his hand on her arm.

"Well?" he said in a loud voice, to be heard above the storm.

"I think it's somewhere around here," she shouted back. "I remember seeing the lights from those cottages." She pointed.

Powell could just make out the ghostly shape of the towans off to the left and some faint lights wavering up ahead. "Right. Lead the way."

She turned sharply right and began to zigzag systematically down the beach, like a spaniel quartering through a woodcock covert, her torch beam playing crazily over the rocks. After what seemed an interminable interval the light suddenly stopped moving. "Over here!" she cried.

Powell hurried toward the light and arrived, slightly out of breath, at her side. He began to say something, but his gaze was drawn to the pool of water at her feet and the object thus illuminated.

It was the most fantastic thing he had ever seen. Lying partially submerged in a shallow rock pool was a human torso, or rather what was left of one. Headless, with a gaping dark cavity where the neck should have been, the left arm missing, and both legs gone cleanly below the knees. Ribbons of decomposing flesh hung from the exposed rib cage on the left side of the body; the skin on the right side of the chest looked more or less intact, although it was wrinkled and puffy like an overripe plum. And covering about half of the corpse above the waist was what appeared to be a woolly growth of dirty gray fur. It was evidently the body of a woman, albeit an inexplicably hirsute specimen, and it had obviously been in the water for a considerable length of time.

Powell blinked slowly to make sure his senses weren't deceiving him. "Shut your torch off," he said in an unnaturally loud voice. He hadn't noticed that the wind had abated somewhat, making shouting no longer necessary. He pulled back the hood of his rain jacket. It had stopped raining.

Jane Goode complied without speaking. Then she froze, transfixed by the wondrous sight before her. "Good God," she said.

There was no mistake about it. The corpse was glowing faintly with a preternatural blue-green light that seemed to emanate somehow both from within and without, like a ghastly aura of corruption. Powell felt the adrenaline rushing through his body as his mind raced wildly. There had to be a logical explanation for it. He knew that certain marine organisms gave off a kind of light; once, while sailing at night in the North Sea, he had seen the plankton sparkling in the water like a million stellar nebulae. Perhaps such organisms could attach themselves to a floating object and create a sort of phosphorescent effect, he speculated doubtfully, but it didn't seem very likely.

Without speaking, he knelt down beside the pool and began to examine the body, as well as the surrounding sand and rocks. From time to time he flicked on his torch for a few seconds and then extinguished it again.

Eventually, his companion could stand it no longer. "Would you mind telling me what in heaven's name you're doing?"

"Technical stuff," Powell rejoined dryly.

"Remember who found the bloody thing," she said. A nervous pause. "You don't think it's radioactive or anything, do you?"

Powell ignored her. "It's odd," he said. "It doesn't seem to have much of a smell."

She sniffed noisily. The only distinct odor she could detect amongst the general smell of salt and muck was the antiseptic iodine note of sea wrack, patches of which were scattered here and there over the rocks. "So?"

He shrugged. "Given the state of decomposition, one would have thought ... I don't know, perhaps it has something to do with the salt water. Can you find me a stick?"

"What?"

"I need something to scrape up a sample with."

"Oh, all right." She shone her torch on the beach around her boots and then stooped to pick something up. "Will this do?" She handed Powell a thin piece of driftwood about six inches long.

"Perfect. Shine the light here." He rummaged in his pocket and retrieved a small glass vial. He unscrewed the cap and then, using the stick, scraped some fragments of sand and debris from the body into the vial; he screwed the cap on and placed it back in his pocket. "Right. We'd better get back. The tide's on its way out, so it should be all right to leave the body here for a little while—"

Suddenly there was a flash and the whine of a film-winding mechanism. After taking half a dozen photographs, Jane Goode said brightly, "Well, so much for the Riddle of Penrick."

Powell got slowly to his feet and shone his torch in her face. "Surely not, Ms. Goode."

"What do you mean?"

A melodramatic pause. "The riddle, I think, is who she is. And how she died."

She blushed profusely. The thought hadn't occurred to her until that moment. She raised a hand to shield her eyes. "Would you mind shining that thing somewhere else?" she asked irritably.

With Powell leading the way this time, they set off back to the Wrecker's Rest, retracing their steps as closely as possible. At the point where they had first left the beach path, Powell built a little cairn of rocks. He whistled tunelessly as he worked. A few stars were glimmering through a tattered shroud of clouds.

When they arrived back at the guesthouse, Powell briefed Sergeant Black and then rang up Chief Inspector Butts in St. Ives to inform him of their gruesome discovery. He made arrangements to have the body attended to that night and for the scene-of-crime lads to come out first thing the next morning.

Half an hour later Powell and Jane Goode, having just narrowly escaped the clutches of an aggressively inquisitive Mrs. Polfrock, were sitting down at a table in the Head. A fire crackled in the grate, flickering cozily on the dark oak beams. A sprinkling of other patrons (a mixture of locals and visitors by the looks of them) added to the general atmosphere of conviviality, making up for their lack of numbers with the boisterous nature of their conversations. Tony Rowlands was over in a flash to take their order. He hovered overly attentively around Ms. Goode, Powell thought.

"A glass of white wine would be nice," she said. "Any old plonk will do."

Rowlands smiled unctuously. "May I recommend the house chardonnay?"

Powell glanced over the drinks menu. "Fine. A half-liter to start with, please."

"I'm sorry, Chief Superintendent," Rowlands said smoothly, "we only serve wine by the glass. House rules, I'm afraid."

The first rule prescribed the usurious exploitation of one's patrons, Powell presumed. "A glass for Ms. Goode, then, and I'll have a pint of St. Austell," he said frostily.

Rowlands oozed over to the bar and soon returned with their drinks.

Powell raised his glass. "Cheers, Ms. Goode, we've had a good night's work."

She eyed him shrewdly. "First off, it's Jane. Secondly, I'm not about to share the glory. I found the damn thing and that's the way I'll be reporting it. Cheers."

"I beg your pardon?"

"I'm a reporter and this is my, um, scoop."

Powell raised an eyebrow. "Is that so?"

"I'm a freelancer, actually." She took a gulp of wine. "Well, to tell the truth, I'm a novelist. This is just a bit of moonlighting to keep body and soul together."

"A novelist?" Powell was intrigued. "Perhaps I've read one of your books."

She smiled ruefully. "I think that's highly unlikely. I've only written one. *Borders.* It came out last year."

"What's it about?"

"You'll have to buy a copy to find out."

Powell grinned. "I'll do that." He took a sip of his beer, regarding his companion speculatively over his glass. He could not deny that Jane Goode interested him greatly. With her dark flowing hair and sea blue eyes, she was a striking woman, although not what you'd call pretty in the conventional sense of the word. She moved easily and naturally, suggesting a certain sensuous muscularity. It wasn't hard to imagine her hoisting a jib or galloping astride a horse. And a writer, besides. He suppressed a twinge of envy as he considered his own position in the scheme of things—a minor government functionary, when it came right down to it, a small cog in a big wheel going around and around in never-ending bureaucratic circles. He would no doubt leave the world much as he found it—not a book or a painting or poem to mark his passage. Suddenly he colored; he realized that he had been staring at her.

Her eyes sparkled. "A penny for your thoughts, Chief Superintendent."

"Er, it's Erskine."

"Erskine?"

Powell smiled thinly. "Erskine Childers Powell. My old man was keen on sailing and Home Rule."

"I don't understand . . ."

"Erskine Childers was a sailor and an IRA man, as well as a writer," he explained. "He wrote a story about a pair of English sailors playing cat and mouse with the German navy just before the start of the First World War. It's generally regarded as the first spy novel."

"I know it—*The Riddle of the Sands!*" She burst out laughing. "That's rather appropriate under the circumstances, don't you think? Actually, I've never read the book, but I did see the movie. Come to think of it, you do remind me a little of that Foreign Office bloke—the one played by Michael York—Carruthers, isn't it?"

"Oh, yes?" Powell was slightly disappointed; he had always identified more with the swashbuckling Davies.

"I think I'll just call you Powell."

He sighed. "Fine."

There followed a lengthy silence that only Powell found awkward.

Eventually his companion spoke quietly. "It's only just beginning to sink in. That was a human being out there on the beach, not just some sort of . . . curiosity. Do you—do you have any idea how she might have died?"

Powell shrugged. "Hard to say. A boating accident is the first thing that comes to mind. But in this case . . ."

"Yes?"

"Well, it's a bit bizarre, don't you think? Corpses don't normally glow in the dark."

"No, I suppose not."

"We'll be able to make a closer examination tomorrow. In the meantime, it remains a riddle—" he smiled "—more grist for your newspaper mill. Now, another glass of wine?"

"My round, I think."

"They'll drum you out of the reporter's union if you keep that up."

She smiled. "I think we're going to get along just fine, Powell."

Powell's buoyant response was cut short by the arrival of Sergeant Black.

"Mr. Powell, Ms. Goode," he said expectantly.

Powell sighed. "Sit down, Black. How did it go?"

"Butts sent over two of his men to lend a hand. We managed to get the thing bagged and put away for the night in the Polfrocks' shed. It's a bloody long slog with a wheelbarrow, I can tell you. The lads will be back out at the crack of dawn to have a good look around." A pregnant pause.

"I imagine you'll want to turn in early then," Powell said.

"Nonsense!" Ms. Goode protested. "You'll join us for a drink."

Black grinned from ear to ear. "Don't mind if I do, ma'am."

A few minutes later Sergeant Black was contentedly wiping the foam from his upper lip. "You know, sir, this business reminds me of a passage from *The Rime of the Ancient Mariner.*"

Powell rolled his eyes. "Really?"

"Yes, sir." He cleared his throat.

> *"The very deep did rot; O Christ!*
> *That ever this should be!*
> *Yea, slimy things did crawl with legs*
> *Upon the slimy sea."*

"Bravo, Sergeant Black," Jane Goode cried. "Let's see, how does the rest go . . .

About, about, in reel and rout
The death fires danced at night;
The water, like a witch's oils,
Burnt green, and blue and white."

Black looked pleased as punch.

"I'm finding this gathering of the Penrick Literary Society extremely stimulating, but we've got an early day tomorrow," Powell said tersely.

Jane Goode seemed amused. "Speak for yourself."

"I thought you might like to tag along," he said innocently.

She looked at him with a curious expression on her face. "I don't get it."

"It's always been my policy to be completely open with the press."

"Really." She looked doubtful.

Not to be outdone in the literary quotation department, Powell smiled cryptically. *"Truth will come to light; murder cannot be hid long."*

He was unknowingly prescient.

CHAPTER 5

The next day started off on the wrong foot for Powell. He joined Sergeant Black for breakfast in the dining room at eight o'clock, but, disappointingly, Jane Goode was nowhere to be seen. After enduring the full English (consisting of a lonely rasher, an underdone sausage, and a slightly caramelized egg) he vowed never to take another meal at the Wrecker's Rest as long as he lived. And to top it all off, a few minutes later a beaming and effusive Mrs. Polfrock loomed large over their table exuding a miasma of lavender scent.

"Chief Superintendent, I'd like you to meet my brother-in-law, Chief Inspector Butts. He'll soon sort things out, don't you worry."

And thus it was that Powell and Black were introduced to Chief Inspector Alfred "Buttie" Butts of the West Cornwall Division of the Cornwall and Devon Constabulary. Butts was a short, wiry, no-nonsense sort of person, who gave the impression that he knew everything there was to know about anything worth knowing and a few other things besides. To his credit, however, he did appear to be put off by his sister-in-law's lingering presence and took immediate steps to correct the situation.

"Now, Agnes, old girl. If you'll just run along, my colleagues and I have some police business to discuss."

She flounced off in a huff.

"You'll have to excuse my sister-in-law, Mr. Powell. She has a heart of gold, really, but she can be a bit overbearing at times."

Powell though it best to say nothing.

"Yes, well, moving on to the business at hand," Butts continued. "I've got my lads combing the beach where the body was found."

"The exact location may not be that easy to find. I was planning to take you out there myself."

Butts smiled benignly. "I wouldn't worry about it, sir. The tide has been in again this morning. I don't expect we'll find much."

Powell had forgotten about the tide, but he supposed he'd had his mind on other things at the time.

"And besides," Butts continued, "that reporter showed us where to look. Nice bit of skirt, that."

"You are referring, I take it, to *Ms.* Goode?" Powell said icily.

Butts reddened. "Yes, sir. I, er, understand that it was Ms. Goode who found the body."

Powell examined his colleague as if he were some exotic insect climbing up the wall of a specimen jar. "Tell me, Butts, what do you make of all this?"

Butts suddenly became animated. "The whole thing is obviously a crude joke perpetrated by somebody with a twisted sense of humor, and I'm damn well going to get to the bottom of it."

Powell was reminded of Dr. Harris's similar reaction. "Go on," he prompted.

"I used to fish around here as a lad. There are strong currents along this part of the coast and there's no way that a body drifting naturally would continue to wash up on the beach in Penrick Bay night after night. For a few days, maybe, but not two weeks. The bloody thing should have been in Boscastle by now. And then there's the Day-Glo bit."

"What's your explanation, then?"

Butts appeared to consider his words carefully. "Your guess is as good as mine, but it's obviously been done for a purpose. To make a point of some kind."

"Yes, but what point?"

Butts shrugged.

"How about you, Bill? Any ideas?"

Sergeant Black's lower lip protruded thoughtfully. "I think we need to have a closer look at the body," he said.

Powell rubbed his hands together briskly. "Let's do that. I'd like Dr. Harris to have a look at it this morning."

"But he's not a qualified pathologist," Butts protested. "We've got a good man at Treliske Hospital in Truro—"

"Nevertheless," Powell interjected crisply, "Harris *is* a medical man, he's available, and he knows the territory. We can always get a second opinion."

Butts was obviously not pleased. "As you wish, sir."

When Dr. Harris turned up half an hour later in response to Powell's telephone call, Black and Butts carried a black body bag from the Polfrocks' garden shed and deposited it carefully on the ground behind the guesthouse. The sky was a brooding swirl of dark clouds framed by spare, spring branches, and hardly a breath of air stirred. A flock of small birds appeared suddenly overhead, swerving away in unison as if interconnected by invisible control wires. Powell glanced up at the guesthouse. Sergeant Black bent down and unzipped the bag and then meticulously arranged things, as if he were creating a flower arrangement, so that the body, lying on its back, could be viewed to best advantage.

It was not a pleasant sight. Decapitated, the reddish skin wrinkled and blistered and traced with prominent blood vessels, the stump of the neck, left arm, and both legs blackened at the ends, clumps of gray fur around the shoulders and breasts, and the remnants of what appeared to be some sort of orange garment hanging in tatters.

Harris sucked in his breath thoughtfully. "Do you mind if I have a closer look?"

Powell looked solemn. "Be my guest."

Harris removed a pair of surgical gloves from his medical bag and pulled them on. He knelt on the ground beside the body and examined it closely from one end to the other for a considerable period of time. Then he gingerly poked and prodded around the midriff for a few moments. Eventually he stood up, rubbing the small of his back. He smiled grimly. "Well, it's not a ghost, I can tell you that. It's a woman, all right, wearing a life jacket. If you look closely you can see the straps. It's pretty badly torn, but that gray fibrous material is kapok or something like it. Can we turn her over?"

Butts cleared his throat as if to say something, but then he glanced at Powell and apparently thought better of it.

Powell nodded. "Bill, give me a hand, would you?"

Between the two of the them, alternately lifting one

side of the bag and then the other, as if engaged in some ghastly slow motion game of blanket toss, they soon had the body flipped over onto its front. The back panel of the life jacket was more or less intact, with a nylon loop attached to the center just below the remnant of the collar. Through the loop was tied a short length of frayed rope.

"That's interesting," Black ventured.

Powell considered the rope for a moment and then turned to Harris. "Well, Dr. Harris, what do you make of it?"

Harris scratched his head. "Before I offer an opinion, I must emphasize that I am not a forensic pathologist, just a simple GP." A self-satisfied gurgle here from Chief Inspector Butts. "However, certain points are obvious. Others are not so obvious and will require elucidation by someone more qualified than myself." He paused to give Powell the opportunity to respond.

Powell nodded. "Understood. However, I'm confident you'll be able to shed some light on the matter," he added graciously.

"Very well." Harris looked down at the body again. "I'd hazard a guess that it can't have been in the sea for much more than a week or so. There is very little bloating. The marbling effect, that is, the prominent blood vessels, as well as the large bullae, or blisters—there, on the buttocks, for instance—indicate that she's been dead for several days."

Powell frowned. "The so-called Riddle of Penrick was first sighted two weeks ago yesterday. Yet you say this one has only been dead about a week. It doesn't seem to fit."

"I could be wrong, Chief Superintendent. All I can say

is that the general state of decomposition does not appear to be that well advanced. However, in cases like this, a precise determination of the time of death can be problematic. It basically depends on ambient temperature and exposure to sunlight. Given overcast conditions and relatively cool air and water temperatures, one could perhaps stretch it a few days more. I'm afraid that's the best I can do."

Powell considered this information for a moment. "Wouldn't you say, Dr. Harris, that the absence of limbs is striking?"

"That's rather curious, actually. It's not as if the body has decomposed to the point where bits and pieces have started to fall off. Your guess is as good as mine when it comes to the head and left arm—sharks, perhaps? The legs, however, are a bit of a puzzler."

Powell was a bit puzzled himself. Gourmet sharks with a penchant for the upper regions? "What do you mean?"

Harris spoke in a monotone. "The bones look like they've been sawn through cleanly at the knees."

Powell was incredulous. "Sawn? With a saw, you mean?"

"It looks like it." Had Harris's manner stiffened?

"Well, that certainly puts a different light on matters," Powell mused. "And then there's the rope."

Harris shrugged.

Powell suddenly remembered the sample he had collected the previous night. He fingered the vial in his pocket. The Day-Glo bit, as Butts had put it. "When I first saw the body, it seemed to be giving off a faint phosphorescent light, just as it was described in the newspaper reports. Can you think of any explanation?"

"No *natural* explanation, if that's what you mean. If you hadn't seen it yourself, Chief Superintendent, I might have concluded that the power of suggestion was a factor."

"Who wrote the bloody newspaper stories?" Butts muttered.

Powell reddened. "Yes, well, I collected a sample. I'll have it analyzed straight away." His initial doubts about the increasingly mutinous Chief Inspector had begun to blossom into a feeling of full-blown animosity. He turned abruptly to face Sergeant Black. "We'd better get Sir Reggie out here to examine the remains as soon as possible. In the meantime let's get the body to the mortuary in Truro. Chief Inspector Butts will fix it with the local coroner." An incipient snort from Butts at this breach of protocol. "Sir Reginald Quick," Powell added for the benefit of Dr. Harris, "is the Home Office pathologist."

Harris looked at Powell with penetrating blue eyes. (Sailor's eyes, Powell fancied.) "I sincerely wish him luck. And you, as well, Chief Superintendent, because I cannot emphasis strongly enough the necessity of getting to the bottom of this foul business with all due haste or, mark my words, there will be a price to pay!" And with that ominous pronouncement he turned on his heel and strode to his car.

They stood in silence as Harris drove off in a spray of gravel. Something Harris had said stuck Powell as rather curious. He turned toward the guesthouse, his train of thought interrupted. This time he was certain; the curtain in one of the upstairs windows had stirred slightly.

CHAPTER 6

The Head was doing a modest business that night, and from the odd snippet of conversation Powell overheard, the discovery of the body on the Sands the previous night was the hot topic. Tony Rowlands seemed agitated about something as he went about his business delivering drinks and food orders and snapping commands at the long-suffering Jenny behind the bar. Powell sat with Jane Goode and Sergeant Black at what had become their regular table in front of the fire. They had just finished a decent meal of rabbit stew served with local new potatoes.

Jane Goode sipped her wine eagerly. "Now, I'll tell you about mine if you tell me about yours."

"I beg your pardon," Powell inquired modestly. Nothing like a good double entendre to liven up an evening.

She smiled, mildly exasperated. "Your *day*, I mean."

Powell affected an air of disappointment and then drained his pint. "Oh, I see. You first, then."

"Not much to tell really. First thing this morning I showed Butts's men where the body had washed up, but the tide had been in and out, so I don't think they found much. Then I filed a story with my newspaper and spent the rest of the day working on my book."

"That's it?"

"A fairly productive day, I'd say, all things considered. I'd be interested to hear how yours stacks up."

Powell summarized the results of Dr. Harris's examination of the body. "A bit of a riddle," he concluded dryly.

"Careful! I've got a proprietary interest in the use of that word."

"Looking at the thing dispassionately," he continued, "there is still no evidence that a crime has been committed. An accident of some sort is the most likely explanation."

"Dispassionately is the only way to look at anything," Jane Goode said pointedly. "But you can't be serious! Have you forgotten that it's had both its legs sawn off, not to mention the fact that it glows in the dark?"

"There is that," Powell admitted, "and I'm trying to keep an open mind. "But we need to do more forensic work before—"

"You saw it yourself on the beach last night. There's something very weird going on and I don't need some geek in a white coat to prove it to me."

"It's possible that the body has been tampered with, but—"

"Tampered with! That's the understatement of the year. I'm not sure what the proper legal term is, but I thought it was against the law to desecrate a human body. Look, Powell, I think I'm onto something big here and I'm not going to let you or anybody else put me off the scent."

"So *that's* it," Powell rejoined.

"What else did you think?" she snapped back, tossing her head haughtily.

Sergeant Black seemed to be taking considerable pleasure in the proceedings. His head swiveled back and forth as if he were the umpire of a particularly spirited tennis match.

"I'm just saying that we need to look into it a bit more before we rule out the more obvious explanations. I've initiated inquiries to see whether there have been recent reports of missing women anywhere in the country or any marine accidents off the south and west coasts."

She seemed to accept Powell's peace offering and signaled to Tony Rowlands for another round. "I'm sorry—I guess I'm just a bit tense. This deadline is killing me. I should be up in my room writing."

"You know what they say, Ms. Goode: all work and no play . . ."

"Keeps the wolves at bay," she concluded, slurring her words slightly. "And I thought I told you to call me Jane."

Powell smiled. "Yes, ma'am—I mean, Jane."

She turned to Sergeant Black. "What do you think, Bill?"

Black regarded her with fatherly goodwill. "I'm thinking that I'd very much like to read your book, ma'am."

"You can call me Jane, too, if you like."

"Er, I'm more comfortable with Miss Goode, if that's all right with you, ma'am."

"Suit yourself." She yawned hugely. "I think it's past my bedtime—"

She was interrupted by a commotion in front of the bar. Tony Rowlands, his face an unhealthy shade of red and eyes bulging, was shouting at a slight, unshaven man who had the dark, slightly cadaverous good looks characteristic of many of the locals. "Don't you threaten me, you little bastard! Now get out or I'll break your bloody neck!"

The smaller man swayed unsteadily. "Tha's right, have it yer way. But I'll be back in my own good time, don't yer worry." And with that he wove his way precariously amongst the tables, muttering under his breath, and was gone.

Rowlands stood where he was, breathing heavily for several seconds. Suddenly, he seemed to become conscious of his surroundings, and his eyes swept the room wildly, as if to say, What are you lot staring at? Then he turned abruptly and disappeared through the swinging doors that led to the kitchen, leaving Jenny Thompson behind the bar to fend for herself.

There were a few whispered remarks and polite coughs, but eventually chairs scuffed and glasses clinked as the atmosphere in the pub returned to normal.

Sergeant Black caught Powell's eye, a quizzical eyebrow raised.

Powell got to his feet. "I'll settle up." He walked over to the bar. "A bit of excitement this evening, Jenny," he remarked casually.

"Whatever turns you on, Chief Superintendent."

"Who was that bloke anyway?"

She shrugged. "One of the locals. Nick Tebble, his name is."

"A regular, is he?"

Her eyes narrowed suspiciously. "He comes in here once in a while. Why do you ask?"

Powell smiled. "Force of habit. Does he usually carry on like that?"

"Who?"

"Tebble." Careful. There was the possibility that the relationship between Thompson and Rowlands was not just a professional one.

Jenny laughed carelessly. "He keeps to himself mostly, usually drinks alone. Tonight he just seemed to be in a bad mood. He must have said something to set Tony off like that," she added, as if by way of an excuse.

"Ah, well, all in a night's work, I imagine, dealing with patrons who've had a few too many," Powell said. He tipped her generously. "Thank you, Jenny. Until tomorrow."

She fingered the note cautiously. "Ta."

Back at the guesthouse, after bidding his companions good-night, Powell wandered downstairs with the vague intention of perusing the Spartan library in the Residents' Lounge, hoping for more than a Reader's Digest omnibus. It was still early and he needed to unwind before he'd be able to sleep. He turned left at the bottom of the stairs and walked down the hallway, treading cautiously on the creaking floorboards as he had no desire to arouse Mrs. Polfrock. In fact, he had scrupulously avoided her since he and Sergeant Black started taking their meals elsewhere. He could hear a television blaring in a distant room and there was the lingering odor of fried fish. He shuddered. He stopped at the first doorway on the right. The door to the lounge was closed, a sliver of light visible through the crack underneath. He tried the knob; it turned, but the door appeared to be fastened on the inside. Mildly surprised, he tried a little more vigorously, the door rattling slightly on its hinges. There was a muffled scuffling inside the room, followed by a thump, a stifled oath, and then silence.

Mysterious bodies washing up on the beach and now things that go bump in the night. Best to leave well enough alone, he thought. As he retraced his steps he briefly considered a stroll along the beach but decided on second thought that he'd better turn in; he had a busy day planned for tomorrow. He went up to his room and tried to get through to Marion in Canada, but there was no answer. Later, as he lay awake in bed, he couldn't help wondering what Jane Goode was doing.

The next morning, after a brief tête-à-tête with Sergeant Black at a pleasant little teahouse overlooking the harbor, which Black had discovered the previous day (partially redeeming himself in his superior's eyes), Powell was treading the springy turf of the coastal path that traverses the high clifftops along much of the north coast of Cornwall. Thank God for the National Trust. Just ahead was Towey Head; on his left were lush green fields crisscrossed by dry-stone walls crowned with tamarisk bushes, their trunks and branches bent to leeward and distorted by the prevailing southwest wind. To his right the blue sunlit expanse of the Atlantic, its edges frayed by jagged rocks into white ribbons of surf that lashed at the cliffs below. Looking back, he could see the narrow strip of the Sands and towans, and in the distance the pastel-colored cottages of Penrick. He wondered if at that very moment Jane Goode was gazing out her window in the Wrecker's Rest contemplating the perfect gerund, or perhaps sitting on one of the benches along the harbor-side working out some nuance of plot.

The path undulated gently. A few tattered clouds drifted across a blue sky; the trilling of birdsong and a fresh sea breeze enlivened his senses. Periodically, in the distance he heard the *pop pop* of a shotgun. Someone shooting pigeons, he guessed. Just ahead, the track veered inland to avoid an eroded section of cliff that formed a narrow valley descending steeply to the sea. At the head of the valley the path intersected a lane, which Powell knew branched off the main Penrick Road about a quarter mile farther inland. The lane plunged between tall hedgerows, and as he walked down it he tried to identify the various wildflowers that adorned the hedges like an intricate mosaic of stained glass. He could only name a few: golden celandine, barren strawberry and wood betony, campion, early purple orchis, and in the damp places pale carpets of marsh marigold.

It struck Powell that the sparse quickset fences that passed as hedgerows in other parts of the country were but poor cousins to the Cornish variety. The hedges between which he now passed were in fact great mounds of earth and stones, perhaps eight feet high and five feet wide at the base, the whole held together by a profusion of grasses, ferns, and flowers. Substantial, uniquely beautiful and enduring, and imbuing a sense of splendid isolation from the rest of the world—much like the popular romantic conception of Cornwall itself. It was hard not to feel a certain empathy for a people who had once traded their tin for the golden crescents and blue stones of ancient Crete, but who were now almost completely dependent on tourists who descended each summer like a plague of locusts. Powell thought guiltily about his own summer sojourns to Bude.

Deplete the fish stocks and close down the mines, force the young people to look for greener pastures elsewhere, and then expose the local traditions to inevitable erosion by the twin tidal waves of modern transportation and communication systems. In the end one was left with a museum piece—something rather quaint, perhaps, but hardly a living culture. Powell smiled to himself. He should run for local office, if they'd have him.

He was perceptive enough to realize that there was something more at the root of his mental meanderings—a vague but persistent sense of insecurity about his own place in the world. He liked to give his old friend Alex Barrett a hard time about the Scot's sense of pride and place and his Celtic traditions. In actual fact, Powell was deeply envious. He, himself, had led the life of a gypsy as a boy, rattling around the world with his parents from one army base to another, never staying in one place long enough to put down roots. Because of this, he suspected he lacked something essential in his makeup—a kind of anchor to hold him fast in life's tempestuous seas. And most unsettling of all in the present circumstances, he usually tended to think about such things just before all hell broke loose in his life.

It was in this pensive state of mind that Powell found himself at the bottom of the lane amongst the straggle of seaside cottages where Dr. Harris resided. A young woman was working in the back garden of the cottage next to Harris's that Powell had attempted to visit previously, a rustic stone building with a corrugated metal roof. It appeared to be older than its neighbors and, along with its various outbuildings, looked generally run-down.

The woman stood up and turned when she heard the gate hinges creak. She wore a slightly tatty but gaily printed frock, which clung to the contours of her slim body. Long bare legs and a pair of mud-caked Wellies. The effect was striking, to say the least. She had a pretty face, but her eyes looked weary, as if she had seen it all before. She brushed a strand of dirty blonde hair from her face with the back of her wrist and stared at him in a boldly appraising manner. "Something I can do for you?"

CHAPTER 7

Powell introduced himself and managed to wrangle an invitation to tea. The interior of the cottage was even more decrepit than the outside. Grimy wooden floors, tiny windows insufficient to brighten the gloom, and between the main living area and the bedroom (there, a glimpse of jumbled bedclothes) a matchbox-thin partition adorned with peeling yellow wallpaper. In a corner in the kitchen there was a gas cooker flanked by two tiny cupboards, a table and two chairs in front of one of the windows, and no sign of modern plumbing.

"Welcome to my castle," the woman said, her voice thick with sarcasm. "By the way, my name's Linda Porter. Can I interest you in something a little stiffer?" She eyed him with a knowing smile.

"Er, tea will be fine, thank you," Powell said. "You have a lovely view here," he added, peering out the window. Various bits of rusted machinery in the front yard and a gaunt group of curlews on the foreshore.

"It's all right, I suppose. If you have time to enjoy it."

A hint of something in her voice as she busied herself with the tea things.

"I understand from Jane Goode that you and your husband grow flowers for a living. It must be an interesting way of life."

She whirled to face him. "Interesting? Is that what you think it is?"

Powell felt embarrassed. "Well, I've never done much gardening myself. My wife, on the other hand . . ."

She laughed bitterly. "Gardening? Does your concept of gardening extend to gales and bulb fly and eelworm and mildew and mice and the constant threat of one's entire livelihood ending up in the compost heap, not to mention buyers who are trying to screw you out of your profit?" As suddenly as she had lost it, she regained her composure. "I'm sorry. That was unfair. It's just that things haven't been going very well lately—with the crops, I mean—and I guess I just needed to let off some steam. Here, I'll get us our tea," she added, as if by way of a distraction.

With her first sip of tea, Linda Porter seemed to mellow. She explained that she and her husband, Jim, were from Manchester; five years ago they'd quit their dead-end jobs, as she put it, pulled up stakes, and come to Cornwall. She'd been a teacher and he an office clerk. (Once bitten, twice shy, Powell wisely resisted the temptation to mention, by way of small talk, that Marion taught anthropology at King's College, thus avoiding a diatribe on the contrasting academic environment that prevailed at the Chunder Road Comprehensive.) They had originally planned to settle on the southwest coast near Gunwalloe, where Jim had heard that you could make a living growing flowers and vegetables for the markets in London and Bristol. They had been unable to find a suitable property there, but then Jim heard about Penrick from an old schoolmate. It was love at first sight, and they had arranged to lease the cottage. The owner turned out to be Tony Rowlands, Powell was interested to learn. They had an acre of garden in the back and leased some clifftop meadows from a local farmer.

It had all seemed very romantic at the time, but a sense of reality rapidly set in. First off, the north coast of Cornwall was *not* like the southwest coast. Exposed as they were foursquare to the Atlantic, they soon learned that growing ornamental flowers was, at best, a marginal and backbreaking proposition. Daffodils were hit-and-miss due to the prevalence of late-winter storms; moreover, the bulbs had to be dug up every three years and sterilized in hot water to kill the flies and the worms and then replanted. Anemones were susceptible to powdery mildew and were difficult to pick in warm weather before they became *blown*, or full open, and unmarketable. Violets, on the other hand, were their bread and butter. Cheap and easy to grow, each year's stock consisted of runners from the previous year's plants. Small growers like themselves could manage about four thousand plants on a quarter of an acre. They flowered from the end of September right through April and yielded weekly pickings of twelve dozen bunches for every thousand plants, twenty violets and two leaves making up a bunch. The Porters also grew potatoes and a few hundredweight of broccoli and cauliflower each year for local sale.

Listening to all this, Powell got the impression that the couple was just barely able to eke out a living, and that the strain was beginning to take its toll—on Linda Porter, at least. And he began to wonder about Mr. Porter, who, reading between the lines, seemed to be the primary architect of the Porters' self-sufficiency lifestyle. After hearing her litany of woe, he started to feel slightly guilty about keeping her from her chores, so he maneuvered the conversation around to the reason for his visit.

He told her about the discovery of the body and its likely link to the Riddle, although he got the impression she'd already heard about it through the local rumor mill. When pressed for any information she might have, she became evasive, which surprised him given the penchant she had already displayed for saying what was on her mind.

"I never saw it and I didn't go out of my way to look for it, not like some around here with nothing better to do."

"A woman has died, Mrs. Porter. Can you think of anything, anything at all, something you might have seen or heard that may not have seemed important at the time, but which now, with the benefit of hindsight, might possibly shed some light on the matter?"

"I'll bet you have that speech memorized," she marveled.

He smiled patiently. "The fact remains, the body of a woman has washed up on the Sands, a body that has been, not to put too fine a point on it, messed about with. Aren't you the least bit curious? I know *I* am, and when I get curious I tend to ask a lot of questions."

"That's where you and I differ, then." She suddenly looked bored. "Let's get this straight, I don't know who she is or where she came from, and quite frankly I couldn't care less. Now if you'll excuse me, I've got some potatoes to get in."

Thus dismissed, Powell rose to his feet. There was a sudden clumping of boots at the back door and a tall, gangly young man entered the room, his questioning eyes darting from Linda Porter to Powell and then back again. He looked like a schoolboy in need of a holiday.

She sighed heavily. "Relax, Jim, it's only the cops. Chief Superintendent Powell, meet my husband, Jim of the Jungle." If this was an inside joke, her husband didn't seem to appreciate it.

The two men exchanged greetings in a stilted manner, and then Powell took his leave. As he walked next door to pay a social call on Dr. Harris, he could hear the sound of recriminating voices coming from the Porters' cottage.

Dr. Harris was obviously pleased to see him. "Do come in, Chief Superintendent. Make yourself at home and I'll get us a glass of wine. Not too early for you, I hope?"

Powell smiled. "Sun's over the yardarm, I think." One must respect the nautical traditions. A different vintage this time but as usual, the standard of libation at the Harris household was excellent. "I've just had a chat with your neighbors, Mr. and Mrs. Porter."

Harris raised his eyebrows. "Oh, I see. Nice couple, but one feels a bit sorry for them."

"Really?"

"Well, they've chosen a hard sort of life for themselves, haven't they?"

"But they *have* chosen it."

"Yes, but one wonders . . . I mean to say, one shouldn't

really say so, but one gets the distinct impression that the whole thing was mostly Jim's idea and he's not really up to the job. Unfortunately, his missus is bearing the brunt of it. I don't suppose it's his fault, really." Harris smiled. "I fancy he's a bit of a romantic—not at all practical like you and I, Chief Superintendent. The poor chap is not very handy, you see. He'll spend days trying to do a simple repair job on his rotary cultivator while his wife toils away in the fields. I lend a hand whenever I can, but I'm not getting any younger. Believe me, it would be a hard enough life for someone who had the aptitude for it. If it wasn't for Mrs. Porter, I'm sure they'd have packed it in ages ago."

"Not exactly a recipe for marital bliss," Powell observed.

Harris drained his glass. "I wouldn't know about that. Here, we'd better have another."

His glass replenished, Powell took in the panoramic view commanded by Dr. Harris's sitting room window. On an isolated rock at the base of Towey Head a shag was stretching its wings out to dry. To the right he could see all the way round to the village. The wind had freshened and was whipping up storm caps in the bay. A blue-hulled fishing boat, gay with red trim and piled high with lobster pots, was making its way into the harbor. It occurred to Powell that very little of the comings and goings in Penrick Bay could escape the attention of Dr. Harris and his antique telescope. He turned to his host. "You know, I think I'd quite fancy a bit of sailing. You mentioned before that you had an Enterprise; do you think I might borrow it for an afternoon?"

Harris beamed. "I'd be absolutely delighted! Anytime, anytime at all."

"Would you be interested in coming along? Do you good."

His host shook his head regretfully. "I think not, thanks all the same." His thoughts seemed elsewhere.

"Mrs. Porter informs me that she and her husband lease their cottage from Tony Rowlands," Powell observed casually.

"He owns most of the properties along the bay, including this one. Bought it all from one of the mining companies years ago."

"Tony's done all right for himself."

Harris smiled. "There are a few essentials in life, and publicans have the market cornered on one of them."

Powell rose to leave. "Well, I'd best be shoving off. Thanks once again."

"Not at all, Chief Superintendent; the pleasure has been all mine, I can assure you."

As he made his way back to the village along the beach path, Powell had much on his mind: Mrs. Porter, for a start—a bit of a firebrand, that one—and Mr. Porter was not exactly as he'd imagined him. Then there was the breathtaking depth of Dr. Harris's wine cellar and the rather curious fact that not once during their conversation had he inquired about the investigation.

Later that afternoon Powell and Black drove into Portreath for a bit of a break from the normal routine. They had got into the habit of convening in the Head before dinner to compare notes, and again after dinner, come to that, since there was no obvious alternative. The

Residents' Lounge of the Wrecker's Rest was clearly out of the question. However, it had occurred to Powell that it might be prudent to locate an alternate bolt-hole, somewhat removed from Penrick, to dispel any suspicions amongst the ratepaying public of that fair village that the Metropolitan Police Service was comprised entirely of dipsomaniacs.

Thus it was that they found themselves snugly ensconced in a seaside pub, sampling the local bitter and looking out at a heaving gray sea. A group of surfers clad in black wetsuits and looking for all the world like a troupe of trained seals were riding the waves onto the beach.

"Looks bloody cold," Sergeant Black remarked with studied detachment.

"Good Lord! Do you see that blonde?" Powell exclaimed.

Black smiled indulgently. "When one gets to be my age, sir, one begins to realize that there are other things in life."

Powell snorted. "Such as?"

Black turned pink. "Er, reading good books, like."

Powell laughed. "Don't get me wrong; I like a good read as well as the next man—a naughty bit of Chaucer, for instance—but I am, alas, a victim of my endocrinology."

"Sir?"

"Hormones, Black, hormones! The biochemical basis for love and sex."

"There's more to it than just chemicals, surely, sir."

"I wouldn't bank on it. I have it on reliable authority that even one's philosophy of life is a function of the concentration of serotonin in the little gray cells. Whether one is an optimist or a pessimist, whether one believes in the nobility of human existence or subscribes to the nasty, brutish, and short version. Simply a matter of brain chemistry."

"But love, sir?" Black looked concerned.

"Never mind, old son, nothing another pint won't put right."

Sergeant Black sat without speaking for a moment, his furrowed brow indicating a state of deep concentration. Suddenly his expression brightened and he spoke in a triumphant voice:

> *"Yet all love is sweet,*
> *Given or returned. Common as light is love,*
> *And its familiar voice wearies not ever.*

Mr. Shelley can't be wrong, sir," he concluded matter-of-factly.

Powell smiled ruefully. "You are an unabashed romantic, Bill, and I envy you." He drained his glass. "My round, I think. Then we had better get down to business."

The pints arrived and Powell reviewed the facts of the case. Sixteen days ago a mysterious apparition—the so-called Riddle of Penrick—first appeared on the Penrick Sands. Jenny Thompson, the barmaid at the Head, may have been the first one to see it. Eyewitness accounts varied slightly but were consistently fantastic: half-human, half-beast, a headless female with a luminous aura, and so on. The sightings always occurred at night and seemed to be concentrated on the section of beach between the village and Towey Head, which was rather curious when one thought about it. As far as they knew, there had not been one sighting along the northeastern half of Penrick Bay. Two nights ago, Jane Goode had discovered a body on the beach that fit the general description of the Riddle, and Powell, himself, was able to confirm that this was no ordinary corpse they were dealing with. Dr. Harris's preliminary examination had revealed at least two noteworthy points. Firstly, the legs had been amputated; secondly, based on the visible extent of decomposition, the unidentified female had probably not been dead for much more than a week, the problem being that the Riddle had been sighted on a regular basis for slightly over two weeks now. Yet it seemed inconceivable that the two were not one and the same. One could only hope that Sir Reggie would be able to make sense of it all. The fact that the deceased wore the remains of a life jacket was suggestive, and Powell was certain that his inquiries regarding missing persons would soon bear fruit. He had also asked Chief Inspector Butts to have his men conduct a thorough search of the towans for articles of clothing or anything else of interest.

"The first priority is to ID the body, which could be difficult, and then, if possible, determine the cause of death," Powell concluded, examining his empty glass as if it were a crystal ball that might provide enlightenment. He looked up at Sergeant Black. "Have I overlooked anything?"

Black frowned thoughtfully. "I don't think so, sir. You've pretty well summed it up. As you requested, I talked to Ms. Goode and got the names of all those who reported sightings, at least those she's interviewed for her newspaper articles. I also asked around the village on my own. So far I've identified seven witnesses, including Jenny Thompson and Ms. Goode. I haven't been able to come up with anything original yet, but I still have a few more people to track down. All in all, sir, I get the impression that the locals aren't that keen to talk about it. But I did run into one bloke who might be worth talking more to, a fisherman name of Colin Wilcox. He seems quite knowledgeable about the local tides and currents."

Powell nodded. "That's the crux of it, I think; where did our body come from and how did it end up on the Penrick Sands?"

"There is one more thing, sir. When I mentioned that people seemed a bit closemouthed about recent events, Wilcox volunteered that there were some who linked the Riddle with the unsolved murder of a local girl near here in the Sixties. Girl named Ruth Trevenney. Apparently her body was found washed up on the beach by some hippies."

Powell did not appear to be particularly surprised by this latest piece of information. "We'll have to follow that up" was his only response.

Sergeant Black rose ponderously to his feet and picked up Powell's glass. "Another pint, sir?"

"If you insist, then we'll have something to eat. I noticed a little Indian place in the High Street," he added offhandedly.

Sergeant Black tried not to show his disappointment. He wasn't much for foreign food himself—give him good English fare any day—but he had gotten used to the routine over the years. *Vindaloo*, *korma*, *bhuna*, *tandoori*, and *Balti*, he'd endured them all. He should have known that his superior, like the most depraved sort of opium eater, could not be kept very long from his curry.

When they got back to Penrick, they looked in at the Head; Powell had been hoping to have a word with Jane Goode, but there was no sign of her. At the guesthouse a surly Mrs. Polfrock, having dropped any pretense of civility, indicated that *Ms.* Goode had already gone up to her room. Sergeant Black followed suit and Powell found himself at loose ends. He asked Mrs. Polfrock if she would mind if he used the Residents' Lounge.

"It's all part of the service." She sniffed indignantly. "Just keep the telly turned down. I'm going to bed."

The Residents' Lounge was open and unoccupied. Powell switched on the light and walked over to the small bookshelf beside the window. A dozen or so well-used paperbacks, romance novels mostly; a few titles on local birding and seashell collecting; and the complete auto-biography of Margaret Thatcher. His heart sank. For a reckless moment he considered turning on the television, but he managed to resist the urge. Heaving a sigh, he selected one of the bird books and settled himself into an overstuffed chair. As he thumbed through the color plates of shags and puffins, cormorants and guillemots, he recalled that Mr. Polfrock was a bird-watcher of sorts.

He closed the book and stared straight ahead. Some-thing was scurrying around in the back of his brain, but he couldn't quite put his finger on it. Then it hit him. He had noticed the desk, an escritoire, in the corner of the room on previous occasions and had thought nothing of it. It was just another piece of furniture, although a bit classier than the rest. It was only now that he realized what it was. He had seen them advertised in the glossy sporting catalogues he liked to drool over—the ones with the matched pairs of hand-built side lock shotguns that cost more than his annual salary. He got up and walked over to it. He tried one of the drawers; it wouldn't budge. It appeared to be part of a false front, as did all the others. He reached around the back and felt for the mechanism. There was a soft *click* and the front of the escritoire opened as a unit, revealing a steel door fitted with a combination lock. Just as he had guessed, it was a safe of the type used for storing guns. He held his breath and pulled the handle on the lock. The safe was unlocked and the steel door swung open.

There was one shotgun in the baize-lined compartment—a cheap single-barrel model—and stacks and stacks of magazines. The titles were mostly in French, but judging from the photographs on the covers, the subject matter did not require any translation. Powell had stumbled onto George Polfrock's porno stash.

Feeling a bit furtive about it, he selected a few magazines and began to leaf through the glossy pages of photographs, which had clearly been shot with a clinical rather than an artistic sensibility. It appeared that old George had a predilection for large dominant ladies wielding colonic irrigation nozzles (Powell tried *not* to think about Mrs. Polfrock) as well as alarmingly young-looking girls done up like French maids. Although he personally hadn't much use for psychoanalysis, he couldn't help wondering what a therapist might make of Polfrock's tastes in erotica.

As he examined the stacks of magazines more closely,

it became clear that the material had been further organized, with a librarian's precision, according to the general anatomical theme of each publication. After he had seen enough, he took some pains to rearrange the magazines at random, then he closed and locked the safe door and secured the false front of the escritoire.

He smiled as he turned off the light. That should get the little bugger going.

CHAPTER 8

At seven twenty-two the next morning Sir Reginald Quick arrived in the cathedral city of Truro on the Inter-City Sleeper from London. Powell and Black met him at the station, a bear of a man with an unruly mop of white hair and an animated red face that made him look like he was constantly on the verge of some vascular catastrophe. He had a stentorian voice that had put the fear of God into more than one inexperienced policeman.

"What do you call this hour, Powell? I call it uncivilized! Do you think I can sleep on these damn trains? Privatize the lot of them, then we'll see some bloody service, by God!"

"Good morning, Reggie," Powell said cheerfully. (The renowned Home Office pathologist refused to be called Sir Reginald by those he was on reasonable terms with— "too damned stuffy!") "You know Bill Black, of course."

Sir Reggie scowled. "I need a cup of coffee."

They located a small cafe near the station.

Powell attempted to smooth the waters. "You know I wouldn't have dragged you out here if I didn't think it was necessary. This is not your run-of-the-mill Jane Doe case."

Sir Reggie grunted. "All right, you've piqued my interest. Did you know that the local coroner has already complained about us sticking our noses in? My initial reaction was *screw* him. But you'd better fill me in, sparing not the slightest detail, before I change my mind."

Powell grinned and proceeded to put Sir Reggie in the picture, with the occasional pointed question from the pathologist.

"Well, something is not bloody right, that's clear enough," Sir Reggie concluded when Powell finished. "Have you sent that sample of yours off to the lab yet? No? Then let's have a look at it, man!"

Powell handed the vial over.

Sir Reggie held it up to the light, peering intently at the contents. "Could be, it just could be," he muttered.

"Would you care to enlighten us?" Powell said.

"Not particularly. Unlike you detective chaps, I never speculate. I only pronounce the truth. When I know for certain, I'll tell you."

Powell bit his tongue. Unlike you and your coterie of boffins, he felt like saying, we poor working sods don't have the luxury of living in an ivory tower. But he was satisfied so far. Sir Reggie had taken the bait and seemed securely hooked. And if anyone could get to the bottom of this business, he could.

A few minutes later, they dropped Sir Reggie off at the hospital and then proceeded to the police station in Tregolls Road. There was a message from Butts waiting for them. Powell rang up the Coastguard Regional Rescue

Coordination Centre in Falmouth and was put through to the Operations Centre. He spoke to the watch officer to whom his earlier inquiry had been referred. Apparently a young woman had gone overboard from a motor launch off Torquay a little over three weeks ago. She was still missing and presumed drowned. Though clearly the most promising lead so far, the timing didn't quite seem to fit. He spent the next half hour interviewing the coastguard officer on the subject of ocean temperatures, tides, and currents in the English Channel and along the north coast of Cornwall. When he was done, there was still an hour or so to kill, so Powell had Black drop him off at Truro Cathedral, while the sergeant went off in search of a bookstore. At twelve-thirty Black returned to pick him up and they drove to the hospital to collect Sir Reggie.

"I must have my lunch!" Sir Reggie roared as he piled into the car. "And none of your damn curry, Powell! A goodly wedge of Melton Mowbray is what I need!"

Sergeant Black smiled happily and looked for the nearest pub. Here was a man after his own heart.

Sir Reggie wiped his thick lips with the back of his hand. "That was bloody marvelous and if you're not going to have that pasty, I will."

Powell pushed the local variety of meat and vegetable pie over and watched as Sir Reggie made short work of it, washing it down with a half-pint of bitter. Sir Reggie leaned back in his chair and belched.

"Now, then, what can you tell us?" Powell said. With Sir Reggie, the direct approach was usually best. Unlike many scientific types who perceived themselves as being superior to lesser mortals, Sir Reggie tended not to pontificate or obfuscate, and he was generally happy to share his knowledge with anyone he considered in possession of the wit to appreciate it.

"As you said, an interesting case," he began. "First off, I can tell you that dental records won't help us very much. Ha. Ha."

Powell and Black laughed politely.

"We're dealing with a female, approximately five feet four inches, in her early to midthirties," he continued, serious now. "There's not much to go on by way of an ID. No distinguishing features. Fingerprints are going to be a bit ticklish given the state of decomposition. The flesh of the right hand is more or less intact, but the skin has loosened considerably from exposure to the elements." He selected a soggy chip from his plate and chewed on it thoughtfully. "And *adipocere* has set in."

"Adipocere?" Powell and Black said in unison.

"A waxy deposit that sometimes appears subcutaneously in bodies that have been immersed in water. It causes the ridges that form fingerprints to disappear. One can, however, peel the skin from the fingertips and occasionally get a good print or two. I've had a go with this one, so we'll see what the chaps in Fingerprint Section can do with it. But the exercise will only yield a useful result if her prints are on record somewhere, which, from a statistical point of view, is highly unlikely."

Powell nodded. "Any indication of the cause of death?"

The pathologist shrugged. "No obvious signs of foul play. My instincts tell me that we're dealing with a drowning, but then there's your little sample to consider. Occasionally you chaps do contribute something useful to these investigations."

Powell smiled. "We aim to please."

Sir Reggie rummaged around in the pocket of his tatty tweed jacket and eventually extracted Powell's vial. He next produced a well-used handkerchief and spread it out on the table. He removed the cap from the vial and tapped the contents onto the handkerchief. Before Powell could protest, he said, "Don't worry, I've kept a portion aside for a legal sample. Here, have a look at this."

Powell examined the tiny heap of material: a mixture of sand, unidentifiable debris, and several clumps of black fiber or hair, as far as he could tell. He hadn't paid much attention to it previously, content to leave such matters to the lab analysts. Sergeant Black leaned over to have a closer look.

Sir Reggie peered at the sample. "See this black stuff? I've had a look at it under a microscope. Know what it is?" He stared critically at Powell as if the chief superintendent were a fresh-faced medical student.

"I don't have a microscope, and I prefer not to speculate."

Sir Reggie snorted. "Well done, Powell; there's hope for you yet. But don't pass it off too lightly—it's the key to your mystery, or at least part of it. Those black strands are the rhizomorphs of a fungus, *Armillaria mellea*. It causes wood rot, but that's not its most interesting quality. *Armillaria mellea* exhibits a curious property known as bioluminescence." He paused for effect. "In other words, the bloody stuff glows in the dark!"

Powell felt a surge of energy pass through him. "I don't understand—it couldn't grow in the sea, could it?"

"Of course not. Its natural habitats are woodlots and lumberyards. Luminous wood has been known since Pliny's time," Sir Reggie continued. "We now know that it's the fungus growing in the decaying wood that actually gives off the light. As long as it's kept moist and is actively growing, it will give off a fairly strong light, which in the case of *Armillaria* has a slight bluish green quality. During the war, pieces of infected wood along roads where timber was hauled, or in lumberyards, were occasionally reported to the authorities at night by people who suspected they might be signaling beacons or incendiary devices planted by the enemy. Fascinating, don't you think?"

"Fascinating. But how does a corpse washed up on a beach in north Cornwall get contaminated with a luminous wood-rotting fungus?"

"Don't ask me. You're the detective."

"Would the stuff survive in salt water?"

"I'm not a bloody mycologist," Sir Reggie said gruffly, "but my guess would be no, at least not for long."

"You mentioned that the fungus gives off a fairly strong light; the body was glowing quite faintly when I saw it—I thought I was imagining it at first."

Sir Reggie frowned. "The conditions would have to be just right—it would have to be pitch-black, for one thing. And didn't you say it was raining on the night in question? Some of it may have washed off."

"Is it possible that someone deliberately doctored the body with the fungus? Sprinkled it with the stuff, or something like that?"

"Anything's possible."

Powell shook his head skeptically. "Someone running around Cornwall scattering luminous fungus like bloody fairy dust. It doesn't make any sense. The Riddle was reported independently by several different people; they can't all be in on it. So whoever is responsible would have to get to the body first, tart it up with the fungus, and then bugger off, leaving it for the next passerby to stumble on. And this would presumably have to be repeated, as the stuff would wash off when the body drifted out with the tide again. Unless . . ."

"Yes?"

"When I know for certain, I'll tell you."

Sir Reggie smiled carnivorously. "I suppose I deserved that. In any case, it is a bit of a puzzler, and it gets even more interesting."

"What do you mean?"

"Fixing the time of death is not an exact science at the best of times; I sometimes think that black magic is a better description of the process involved. Nonetheless, it's my opinion that your Riddle has been dead for longer than it might appear at first glance. Corpses basically decompose in two ways," he went on to explain, "from the autolytic action of the body's own enzymes and from putrefaction caused by bacteria escaping the digestive tract. Immersion in cold seawater and limited exposure to sunlight has evidently slowed the rate of decomposition in this case. A superficial examination of the body would suggest a period of perhaps seven or eight days since the time of death. However, if one confined one's attention to the condition of the internal organs, which are pretty far gone, one would be persuaded to place the time of death considerably earlier, fourteen to sixteen days ago, perhaps."

"I'm given to understand that the mean ocean temperature off Cornwall at this time of year is about forty-five degrees," Powell observed.

"The rate of decomposition slows considerably below fifty degrees, still . . ." Sir Reggie frowned. "It's almost as if the bloody thing has been partially embalmed in some fashion. And from the outside in, which is not the usual way of doing things."

Curiouser and curiouser. Then Powell remembered how he'd been struck by the absence of a strong odor when he'd first examined the body. He mentioned the fact to Sir Reggie.

The pathologist nodded. "That fits, although it's getting bloody ripe now, I can tell you. In any case, I've ordered some tests. I'll let you know if I come up with anything earthshaking."

"What about the legs? Dr. Harris thought that they'd been amputated with a saw."

Sir Reggie laughed uproariously, as if this were the funniest thing he'd ever heard. "Your Dr. Harris is a very astute chap," he said, wiping his eyes with his handkerchief and sending the flotsam and jetsam that had comprised Powell's sample flying in all directions. "The majority of his conclusions were substantially correct, but on that particular point he was dead wrong. Sharks probably chewed 'em off first, then the abrasive action of the sand finished the job, smoothing off the ends of the femurs as the body moved up and down the beach with the changing tides. So the culprit is not a hacksaw, but rather a piece of sandpaper. Ha ha!"

Powell and Black looked at each other.

Sir Reggie consulted his watch. "Now, then, my train leaves at three twenty-four. If you drop me off at the station now, I'll have time for a quick snooze. And I'd advise you chaps to hop to it; you've got your work cut out for you."

Powell was on the verge of mentioning the woman reported drowned off Torquay, but decided he'd better wait until he'd seen the official coastguard report. For the time being, he preferred to let Sir Reggie work things out for himself.

As they sped along the A30 past prosperous-looking farms, it occurred to Powell that they had more on their plates than they'd originally bargained for. Not murder, perhaps, but something very peculiar nonetheless. And nothing they had learned so far was inconsistent with the conclusion that it was in fact the Riddle of Penrick lying on a slab in the Treliske Hospital morgue. He turned to Sergeant Black. "As soon as we get back, I'm going to have a word with that fisherman of yours, Colin what's-his-name?"

"Wilcox, sir."

"Right. Tell me, what do make of Sir Reggie's revelations?"

Black frowned. "I think if we can figure out the *why*, the *how* will fall into place, sir. I keep thinking about what Wilcox said about the murder of that girl in the Sixties."

Powell nodded. A detective-sergeant on the same

wavelength as his super is a gift from heaven. "I'll have to ask Buttie about it. He's lived around here all his life; he should be familiar with the case. The murdered girl's father, Roger Trevenney, still lives near Penrick. According to Dr. Harris he's not very well, so I'm reluctant to bother him unless it's absolutely necessary." He sighed. "And there's no reason to suppose there's any connection at this point."

Black nodded.

When they got back to Penrick, the village was cloaked in a dense fog that blotted out the sea and everything else more than fifty feet away.

Sergeant Black pulled up at the Wrecker's Rest and got out.

Powell slid over into the driver's seat. "I'll see you later."

"Right." Black waved as the car bearing his superior disappeared into the mist.

Up the hill and then left at the church, according to Black's directions. Colin Wilcox lived in an isolated house located about a half mile northeast of the village but nearly a mile away by road. This was the less frequented stretch of the Sands enclosed by the small promontory that formed the northerly limit of Penrick Bay. The beach was narrower and rockier here and generally less hospitable to swimmers and boaters. The northern entrance to the bay was guarded by three black pinnacles (offshore stacks to the geomorphology types), shown officially on the sea charts as Parthenope, Ligea, and Leucosia, and known locally, if imprecisely, as the Mermaids. (They were Sirens, actually.) In any case, they had claimed many a boat in the old days. It was said that at extremely low tides a barnacle-encrusted keel could be seen amongst the rocks. None of which, however, was evident to Powell that afternoon as his car crept through the fog along the winding clifftop road, with an ever-present sense of the drop to the rocks and sea below. The visibility was practically zero and the reflected glare of the headlamps only made matters worse. Occasionally he could hear the foghorn sounding forlornly on Godrevy Island.

After what seemed like a never-ending series of hair-raising bends and turns and morbid fantasies ("Scotland Yard Detective Plunges Off Cornish Sea Cliff") Powell was beginning to wonder if he hadn't got himself hopelessly lost. Then suddenly the road turned sharply left and after a short, descending pitch, he found himself stopped on a flattish patch behind the dark shape of a house. A dull yellow glow from one of the windows looked promising, although he had no idea if he was even at the right house. He turned off the motor and got out of the car. He could hear the roar of the sea not far below. Shivering in the damp chill, he walked up to the house and knocked on the door.

A light came on above his head. The curtains parted and a face showed in the window. A few seconds later, the door opened. A tall young man with curly blond hair appeared. "Yes?" he said simply.

"Mr. Wilcox?" Powell asked.

The man nodded, and Powell introduced himself. "I'm sorry for dropping in unannounced, but I wanted to have a word with you about this body we've found. I have reason to believe you can assist us with our inquiries."

The young man smiled disarmingly. "Isn't that what the police officer always says to his primary suspect?"

Powell laughed. "It's not as bad as all that, Mr. Wilcox, I promise you."

"Do come in and have a beer then, Chief Superintendent, and please call me Colin."

Powell followed Wilcox inside. It appeared to be a fairly modern house with an open floor plan, a quarry tile floor in the kitchen and oak parquet everywhere else, modern Danish furniture, and a large picture window facing the sea. Powell imagined that the view on a fine day would be spectacular. Today though, it was all gloom outside. There were times, Wilcox volunteered, when you couldn't see anything for days on end. Powell made some complimentary remarks about the house.

"It was my parents' place," Wilcox explained. "I built the addition myself. The old house still exists, basically the bedrooms, a small study, and a sitting room down the hall there. I lived in California for a few years and picked up some architectural ideas. West Coast Contemporary they call it over there."

"I'm not very handy myself," Powell admitted.

Wilcox grinned. "How about that beer?"

"Great."

When Wilcox returned with two bottles of ale and two glasses, Powell said, "Most people around these parts seem to have an affinity for wine. It's refreshing to run into a beer drinker."

Wilcox winked. "I take whatever's going. Cheers."

"Cheers. Sergeant Black tells me that you're a fisherman."

Wilcox smiled thinly. "That, and a builder in the off-season. My father was a fisherman and his father before him."

"What sort of fishing do you do?"

"A bit of everything. Crabs and lobsters, sport fishing charters in the summer for mackerel, sharks, whatever. In the old days it was pilchards mainly; they used to salt them down in the cellars and export them all over the world. It's not real fishing I do, not like my grandfather, but it's where the money is these days. And the London girls who come out here on holiday seem to appreciate the genuine Cornish article," he added roguishly.

It sounded like a carefree sort of life to Powell. "You have your own boat, I take it."

Wilcox nodded. "I keep it moored in St. Ives."

"I suppose you would get to be quite familiar with the local tides and currents."

"Enough to get by."

"I'll get right to the point, Colin. Something about this business has been bothering me from the start. I understand that this part of the coast is swept by strong currents; assuming that the Riddle and our body are one and the same, I don't understand how something drifting passively in the sea could get caught in Penrick Bay for so long."

Wilcox shook his head in amazement. "You know, you're the first person around here who's even asked the question. It's obvious, isn't it? The whole thing's a put-up job."

"Go on."

"First off, you're right about the currents. We're influenced by the Gulf Stream here and, ignoring local tidal effects, the set is generally to the northeast. I remember once as a kid finding a drift bottle on the beach that had been dumped in the middle of the English Channel by the Ministry of Agriculture and Fisheries as part of a study of tides and currents. There was a little card inside, and if you filled it out saying where and when the bottle was found and sent it in, you got a small reward—five shillings, I think. Over half of the bottles dropped in the Channel drifted round Land's End and came ashore on the north coast, right the way up to Trevose Head. That's about twenty-five miles up the coast from here. So it's not surprising that your body would drift into Penrick Bay with the tides, but it's highly unlikely that it would stay around for more than a day or two."

Assuming of course that it came from somewhere else, Powell thought. "You used the words 'put-up job.' What did you mean?"

Wilcox studied Powell's face carefully before replying. "I mean that someone must have taken an active part in it, dragging the thing onto the beach at night when the tides were right, leaving it where it would likely be found, and then removing it before anyone could get a good look at it. It wouldn't be easy."

The same idea had been running round the back of Powell's brain as an admittedly far-fetched possibility, but hearing someone else articulate it caused a familiar thrill to surge through his body. It was the sensation he experienced when all of his faculties were humming along in tune. "And they'd have to keep it hidden somewhere between times," he mused.

Wilcox pulled a face. "Not a pleasant thought, is it?"

"But why would anybody go to all the trouble?"

"It does seem pretty bizarre."

Wilcox's description of the local currents was consistent with what Powell had been told by the coastguard officer in Falmouth. Time now to get to the real reason for his visit. "You mentioned to Sergeant Black that some people in Penrick were making a connection between the Riddle and the murder of Ruth Trevenney."

Wilcox appeared to hesitate, then he shrugged. "There's been some talk going around. It's no secret."

"What do *you* think, Colin?"

He met Powell's steady gaze. "I can tell you what I know about it, if that would help."

Powell nodded.

"My father told me the story," Wilcox began in a quiet voice. "I was still in nappies when it happened. Ruth Trevenney lived with her father in a cottage up along Mawgawan Beach. He still lives there. He's quite a well-known artist, used to be a leading light in St. Ives before it got too trendy," he added parenthetically. "Anyway, one day Ruth just disappeared. It was in 'sixty-seven, I think—she was sixteen or seventeen at the time. A massive search was undertaken, involving local volunteers, the police, and the coastguard, but to no avail. A few days later, her body washed up on the Sands with its throat slit. The girl who discovered it was high on acid at the time, and it created quite a stir in the media. The police later discovered that Ruth's body had been thrown down an old mine adit that drains to the sea. You can see the opening in the cliff between the Old Fish Cellar and Mawgawan Beach. There was a heavy rain and the body ended up in Penrick Bay. Even today after a good rain, contaminated drainage from the mine workings discharges from the tunnel and stains the sea red. There's some around here that say it's the blood of Ruth Trevenney."

"You mentioned the Old Fish Cellar."

"It's where they used to salt the pilchards down, just past Towey Head."

"Go on."

"The murderer was never found. There were lots of rumors flying around at the time: drug smugglers, the hippies who used to hang out around Mawgawan Beach, you name it. Everyone had their own pet theory, apparently."

"And your father?"

Wilcox did not look up. "I don't remember him voicing an opinion on the subject, and I never asked. I do know that Ruth and her father were well liked around here."

No point in beating about the bush. "So is someone actually suggesting that the Riddle of Penrick is Ruth Trevenney's ghost, or something to that effect?"

Wilcox smiled wanly. "Not in those words exactly, but you have to admit there's an eerie similarity. And we Cornish are a superstitious lot."

"Hmm. Could you draw me a rough sketch showing the relative location of Mawgawan Beach, the Trevenneys' cottage, the Old Fish Cellar, and the mine drainage tunnel, so I can get my bearings?"

"No problem." He went off to search for a pen and paper.

Powell was beginning to weave together in his mind a number of hitherto unrelated threads. A body that glows in the dark like an hallucination, the sensitivity of the local police to an incident that bears a disturbing resemblance to a previous unsolved murder, and the outrage of

Dr. Harris, the friend of Roger Trevenney. Still, a connection with something that happened thirty years ago seemed improbable. More likely it was somebody pulling a prank, as others had suggested. An unfortunate accident somewhere along the coast, the body washes up on the Sands, and some yob takes advantage of the situation. A tasteless joke at best, a misdemeanor at worst. But why couldn't he convince himself? He emptied his glass.

Wilcox returned and drew a map of Penrick Bay and the section of coastline immediately to the southwest. In a neat hand he made various notations on the map. When he was satisfied, he handed it over to Powell.

Powell examined the sketch. "That helps considerably. Thanks." He folded the paper and placed it in his pocket.

"Not at all."

"I won't take any more of your time, Colin, but I may need to talk to you again."

Wilcox smiled. "You know where to find me, Chief Superintendent."

A real charmer, Powell thought as he got into his car. As he turned around in the driveway, he had the feeling that Wilcox was watching him.

CHAPTER 9

The boom swung around and Powell felt the sea surge under the plywood hull as the little Enterprise heeled over and began to pick up speed, the mainsail thrumming in the wind, spray flying from the bow.

"Take in the sheet!" Powell called out to Jane Goode, who had her hands full wrestling with the jib.

"What sheet?" she shouted, her voice edged with panic.

"That line in your hand, the bloody rope, woman!"

"Then why didn't you say so!" she retorted, pulling it through the cleat like he had shown her during their test run in front of Dr. Harris's cottage. But now they were nearly half a mile offshore with nothing between them and North America but water, and the rocks of Towey Head were coming up quickly on their left—er, port side, she corrected herself. And she'd already forgotten what a spinnaker was, or was it a luff?

Powell grinned at her. Hair flying in the wind, her face flushed, she looked wonderful. The last of the morning fog was burning off, and it promised to be a fine day. A fresh westerly was blowing and lines of white horses advanced across a vast blue meadow of sea. What better way to use Colin Wilcox's map to familiarize himself with the local coastline and get the juices flowing besides?

Jane Goode, however, viewed the situation rather differently. A rash acceptance of Powell's proposal in the Head last night, induced by a surfeit of wine, she supposed ruefully; a mighty struggle with Powell to launch Dr. Harris's thirteen-foot sailboat that morning; and now she found herself drenched with spray and hanging on for dear life as the tiny dinghy, leaning over at an alarming angle, sliced through the choppy waves. More than anything else, she was angry at herself, at her own sense of incompetence. She had always considered herself fairly athletic—she had excelled in a number of sports at school and still tried to keep fit biking and jogging. But she was cautious by nature and didn't like to jump into anything new without first doing her homework. If she had wanted to try sailing, for instance, she would have enrolled in a course of sailing lessons, not agreed to go out in a gale in a minuscule boat with a suicidal maniac who seemed intent only on showing off. Men, they were all the same! But she'd be damned if she'd let him get the better of her. Clenching her teeth, she checked that her feet were hooked securely under the toe strap and then hung her rear end out even farther over the gunwale.

Gannets plunged offshore, a pair of gray seals frolicked in their wake, and Powell's spirits soared. He loved the wind and spray in his face. Every faculty finely tuned to the elements and the lively response of the dinghy. If he had been alone he would have whooped for joy. He had almost forgotten what it was like, but he supposed it was like riding a bicycle—one never lost the knack.

Climbing and sailing had been his passions as a young man, but both had fallen to the wayside over the years, victims of the various encumbrances that seemed increasingly to complicate his existence, weighing him down like Jacob Marley's chain. But such thoughts were far from his mind as they came around Towey Head on a beam reach with the wind off their port side.

He turned the dinghy to windward and came around, sheeting in the mainsail until they were sailing close-hauled parallel to the shore about two hundred yards off. "Jane, come back here and take the helm, would you?"

She made her way unsteadily aft, changing places with him, and clutched the tiller in a death grip.

"We're sailing close to the wind now, so keep your wits about you. You want to keep the mainsail sheeted in, but not too tight. If you get into trouble," he added, declining to explain exactly what he meant, "just turn into the wind to slow down and, if necessary, ease the sheet a bit and slacken the sail." He settled himself amidships and began to scan the rocks with a pair of binoculars. "A little to starboard," he directed. And then, "Steady as she goes."

"You're crewing now, so watch it, mate!" she warned.

Powell grinned and gave her a mock salute. "Aye, aye, captain!"

Just beyond the rocks of Towey Head a small cove and a drab stone house set on the shore at the base of the cliffs came into view, a small wooden boat hauled up on the rocky beach. Powell focused the binoculars on the sign over the door, reading the words aloud. "The Old Fish Cellar, *Dulcis Lucri Odor*."

"What does it mean?" Jane said.

"Profit smells sweet." A decent education still very occasionally proved its worth. "It's a relic of the pilchard fishing days; it's where they used to salt the fish down."

"I think that's where that bloke lives—the one who got into the row with Tony Rowlands the other night."

"Really." Powell searched his memory. "Nick Tebble, isn't it?"

Jane nodded. "A bit of a local character, apparently."

"So I gather." Powell consulted Wilcox's map. "That stretch of sand up ahead is Mawgawan Beach." He glassed the rocks systematically for several minutes. The beach gradually fell behind them, more rugged coastline, a low jutting point crowded with piping oystercatchers, and then a small cottage perched above a tiny teacup of a bay. "That must be Roger Trevenney's cottage. He painted the picture of Towey Head that hangs in Dr. Harris's parlor."

"I was admiring it this morning. It's brilliant."

Powell looked at Wilcox's map again. "Somewhere between the Old Fish Cellar and Mawgawan Beach there's supposed to be an opening in the cliff face, an old mine tunnel of some description. I didn't see it; we'd better go back and have another look. Do you think you can handle it?"

She gulped. "Handle what?"

"We need to turn the boat around until we're sailing on a broad reach in the opposite direction."

"A broad reach?"

"With the wind behind us, off our port quarter in this case. Remember?"

"Right. Would you mind running through the procedure again?" She had turned deathly pale.

Powell smiled reassuringly. "We're presently on a starboard tack. We need to gybe, that is fall away from the wind to port, turn the stern through the wind, and establish a port tack with the wind aft. To carry out the maneuver the mainsail has to be completely slackened off then swung around to the other side. Unlike coming around into the wind, gybing is done when the boat is moving at full speed, so the timing can be a bit tricky. And in this case we have to watch that we're not blown onshore."

He neglected to mention that gybing is considered the most difficult of sailing maneuvers and is the point when dinghies are most liable to capsize. However, the winds were moderate and he had concluded by then that his companion was a quick study. And he'd be poised to take over the helm if she got into trouble. He went over the various steps and commands in detail and then asked her to repeat them until he was satisfied that she had the routine down pat. He knelt down and pulled the centerboard up halfway so the boat would slip to leeward at the critical moment, thus lessening the degree of heel and the danger of capsizing. Better to be safe than sorry. He got back into position. "Whenever you're ready," he said.

She positioned her feet apart. "Right." She took a deep breath. "Stand by to gybe!"

"All clear!" Powell sang out.

She slackened off the mainsail while he eased the jib.

The dinghy began to turn before the wind. It seemed to take forever for the boat to come around and all the while they were drifting rapidly toward the rocks. Her heart pounded. She willed herself to move, but her body would not respond. The cliff face loomed about fifty yards off now and she could pick out individual rocks glistening like black fangs amongst the foaming chaos of surf.

"Now!" Powell shouted.

His voice galvanized her into action. Frantically hauling in the mainsheet, she pulled the boom amidships. "Gybe oh!" she cried hoarsely and then pulled the tiller toward her, ducking as the boom swung over. She moved over to the port side, easing the mainsheet. Under Powell's direction, she mechanically trimmed the mainsail and adjusted the tiller, rounding up on a new course heading toward the point of Towey Head. She felt numb, drained of any capacity for further action.

"Well done!" Powell said, grinning boyishly. He felt his muscles beginning to relax. Best not to mention that he had been within a split second of grabbing the tiller. He felt a twinge of guilt; he had to admit that he'd been testing her. Yet all things considered, she had passed with flying colors.

When Jane was able to relax a little, the reality of the situation suddenly struck her. Her face burned as she realized what a close call it had been. "We might have been killed!" she protested.

Powell was already searching the shoreline with his binoculars. "Nonsense," he said in a matter-of-fact manner. "A few more lessons and you'll be well on your way to becoming a sailor."

God, he could be irritating at times! Still, she had to admit to a growing sense of accomplishment. She had overcome her fear and done something she would never have considered attempting on her own. She studied Powell unobtrusively. Slightly past his prime, but still attractive in an understated sort of way. And he exuded a reassuring air of competence, although she sensed something else below the surface. She couldn't help wondering what he was really like underneath the professional veneer . . . She suddenly checked herself. What are you thinking, woman? He's a married man (the ring had not gone unnoticed), and you don't need any complications in your life right now. You've got a book to finish and besides—

"There it is! Directly off the beam, halfway up the cliff face. Do you see it?" He handed her the binoculars.

She manipulated the glasses awkwardly with her left hand, keeping her right hand firmly on the tiller. She examined the sheer face. "Yes, I think so." There appeared to be the dark mouth of a tunnel, too symmetrical to be natural, with a rusty stain streaking the gray granite down to the sea. She lowered the glasses. Once you knew what to look for, the feature was obvious to the naked eye.

"It's an adit, draining one of the old tin mines," Powell explained. "The minerals stain the rock red; I'll tell you a story about it later. For now, why don't we take in the sails and I'll row us in to Mawgawan Beach. I'm feeling a bit peckish, how about you?"

Anything to get her feet on solid ground again, she thought. The sun was beating down now and the wind had died to an intermittent breeze. A picnic lunch on the beach began to look quite appealing. And she could use the opportunity to pry some details about the case from Powell. "Prepare the jib halyard," she ordered crisply.

The beach was enclosed on three sides by towering cliffs. Waves slid languidly onto tawny sand, immaculate white gulls mewed overhead, and a hazy, aquamarine sea stretched as far as the eye could see.

Powell filled Jane Goode's wineglass from the unmarked green bottle that Dr. Harris had provided and then replenished his own. "Is it just me or have you noticed that there seems to be an almost Dionysian abundance of good French wine available in this corner of Cornwall?"

"Who's complaining?"

"Certainly not I, but I'll bet you haven't seen a bottle with a proper label on it. If I had a suspicious nature, I'd think that somebody was smuggling the stuff in by the barrel."

Jane knew from her background research for her book that the north coast of Cornwall used to be notorious for smuggling in the eighteenth and nineteenth centuries, when vast quantities of brandy and tobacco, to name just two of the most valuable commodities, were imported illegally from France to circumvent high import duties. She frowned slightly. "Now that we're all one happy family in Europe, it wouldn't make any sense, would it? I thought you could bring back as much duty-free booze as you wanted nowadays."

"Up to a point, provided it's for personal use. But not everyone can afford to pop over to France for a couple of liters of wine whenever the urge strikes. So there's still a lot of alcohol that gets smuggled in by the lorryful." Powell paused for a sip of what Dr. Harris had accurately characterized as a surprisingly bold merlot. A faint smile. "However, one wouldn't wish to seem impolite by asking. Pass me another piece of that cheese, would you?"

She eyed him shrewdly. "You were going to tell me about that old mine tunnel."

He chewed thoughtfully. "Do you know about Roger Trevenney's daughter Ruth?"

She shook her head. "Is there any reason I should?"

He looked at her carefully. "She was murdered near here in the Sixties. According to some of the locals, there are uncanny parallels between the circumstances surrounding her death and your Riddle."

"I haven't heard that," she said, defensive.

He could not resist a little jab. "Since you're a journalist I naturally assumed . . ."

She flushed angrily. "An amateur, you mean—not a professional busybody like yourself?"

He smiled. "Actually Sergeant Black bumped into a local fisherman who let it slip. They made me take a management course once where I learned that a good leader should be content to bask in the reflected glory of his or her able assistants."

"Do you think you could possibly get on with it?" she said testily.

Powell related the story as it was told to him by Colin Wilcox. "It seems that tunnel in the cliff face drains the very mine where the murderer disposed of Ruth's body. Whenever it rains, the tunnel discharges a flow of rusty water to the sea. The blood of Ruth Trevenney, according to some."

Jane shivered. "Lovely." She paused thoughtfully. "But perhaps that explains it."

"Explains what?"

"When I first started asking questions about the Riddle, people seemed . . . I don't know, sort of reticent. I assumed at the time that they were reluctant to talk about it because I was an outsider, not to mention the fact that the incident had brought a certain notoriety to Penrick. But maybe there was more to it than that; an echo of a past tragedy, the terrible murder of one of their own. I didn't feel comfortable prying, somehow."

Powell laughed. "A reporter with tact; now there's an oxymoron."

"Like a sensitive policeman," she retorted.

"Ouch! I suppose I deserved that." For the first time he was aware of looking into her eyes. He smiled self-consciously. "Truce?"

Jane Goode's gaze was unwavering. "Why not?"

Powell cleared his throat. "Yes, well, getting back to the murder of Ruth Trevenney, any connection with the Riddle has to be considered a long shot at this point, but I suppose it can't be ruled out. At the very least I'll have to review the file on the case." He could already anticipate Buttie's reaction to that particular suggestion, more unwarranted prying by outsiders into local police affairs. "I'd rather not bother Roger Trevenney," he continued. "He's not very well, apparently, and I'd prefer not to open old wounds if I can avoid it."

A hint of sensitivity after all? Perhaps she'd been a little harsh in her judgment. Although it annoyed her to admit it, Powell continued to fascinate her. Absolutely insufferable one minute and something quite different the next. But what exactly? Once again, she couldn't put her finger on it. A certain vulnerability, although one would hardly expect that in a policeman whose sensibilities had no doubt become jaded by . . . There she was, doing it again! Would she never bloody learn? Then she heard the sound of Powell's voice.

"I'd be interested to hear your opinion."

"My—my opinion?"

He nodded. "You basically have all the information I have now. What's your conclusion?"

She eyed him warily. "I'm not sure I want to play a Watson to your Holmes, if that's what you have in mind."

He laughed. "It's not like that at all. I solemnly promise that I will never utter the word 'elementary' in your presence. I simply want to know what you think. You've taken an active interest in this thing from the start; you must have some ideas."

"I'm surprised you'd wish to consult with an amateur," she said skeptically.

"Look, Jane, I'm serious. I'm beginning to get a funny feeling about this business, and I'd appreciate an objective opinion, that's all. I don't know you very well, but I already have good reason to trust your judgment." A twinkle in his eye. "After all, we've gybed together."

She smiled in spite of herself. "I suppose I should feel flattered. But you're right; I have thought about it. Quite a lot, as a matter of fact. Not because I've wanted to—it's kept me from my novel, which I doubt I will ever finish— it's just that the whole thing is so damnably strange. I suppose it's the storyteller in me, but like you I've come to the conclusion that there must be something more to it. Something sinister, I think."

"Those are your words, not mine," Powell rejoined sternly.

She swept the hair from her face in a gesture of impatience. "You know what I mean. Someone has obviously gone to a lot of trouble to pull this thing off. It's not your run-of-the-mill prank. We're dealing with a dead body, after all, not graffiti on someone's garden wall. And you'll have to admit that the glow-in-the-dark fungus was a brilliant touch, no pun intended."

"But why?" Powell mused.

"You're the detective."

"Somebody else has recently made that point." He shook his head, frowning. "Damn it all! My instincts keep leading me back to Ruth Trevenney."

"At least we have one thing in common."

Powell gave her a curious look. "What do you know about the Porters?" he asked, changing mental gears.

She shrugged. "I've chatted with them in the pub a few times. Why do you ask?"

"I met them the other day myself, and I remember you mentioning them."

"You haven't answered my question."

"I'm just curious."

"What do you want to know?"

"General impressions, for a start."

She thought about it for a moment. "Linda seems to do most of the talking. I don't know, they seem nice enough, and they've given me some great stuff for my book. In a way, the story is about them." She was becoming animated now. "You see, it's about this couple—he works in the City and she's in public relations—who tire of their life of endless parties and superficial relationships and decide to pack it all in for a life of genteel self-sufficiency in Cornwall. The idea is sort of romantic, don't you think?

So when I came out here to write the book, you can imagine how thrilled I was to meet the Porters. It's rather like life imitating art."

Genteel self-sufficiency. Life imitating art. Powell spoke carefully, aware that he was treading on dangerous ground. "Have you been out to their cottage, by any chance?"

"No, why do you ask?" she replied guardedly.

"Just asking," he said, discretion being the better part of valor. "Is there anything about them, or the way they relate to each other that strikes you?"

"Why do I feel I'm being interrogated?"

"We're not allowed to use that word anymore."

She wondered what he was getting at, although she thought she had a good idea. "I make a point of not judging people too quickly, even policemen."

"Very funny. I get the impression that they don't get along very well."

"A lot of married couples don't get along very well."

"I'll tell you the thing that struck *me* about Linda Porter. Unlike everybody else around here I've spoken to, she didn't seem the least bit interested in the Riddle or the fact that a woman's body has washed up on the beach not more than a quarter mile from her cottage." There was something else about Linda Porter that he declined to mention, an aura of sexuality that was reminiscent of the chemical pheromone exuded by certain female moths that has the effect of attracting every male from miles around. Powell could picture her in her garden in her green Wellies and very little else.

He suddenly wondered what Marion would think if she knew that he was picnicking with an attractive novelist on a secluded Cornish beach known for its nude bathing. She probably wouldn't give it a moment's thought, he decided; she knew him too well. He sighed and gazed out to sea. The breeze had freshened again, ruffling the surface of the water. "You'd better finish your wine," he said. "We should be getting back."

"Yes, I suppose so." She looked disappointed.

Linda Porter picked up the telephone. "Yes." She sounded bored.

Tony Rowlands was on the other end, his voice tight. "I got your message. I told you not to call me here."

"Afraid little Jenny might get jealous?"

"Don't be ridiculous. I'm busy, that's all. The lunch crowd—"

"Screw the lunch crowd!" she snapped. "Do you expect me to sit here at your beck and call?" She took a deep breath. "Look, sugar, I need you. I want you to come over so we can, um, talk."

"You know I can't get away now, besides I really don't feel up to it. I mean to say, I've got a lot on my mind . . ."

"Nick been in again?"

"Not since the other night."

"What are you going to do about it?"

"About Nick? What do you mean?"

"He's not going to let it lie, you know that."

"He's harmless, really."

She laughed harshly. "Harmless? That's rich."

Rowlands's voice sounded tense. "As long as I give him a bit of work now and then, he's happy."

She gripped the receiver tightly. "He'll never be happy, you know that."

"Look, just leave it to me." Muffled voices in the background. "I've got to go."

"Jim will be away again tomorrow . . ." Her voice pleading now.

"I'll call you later." *Click.*

"You bastard!" She slammed the receiver down. Why did she always get tied up with losers?

She took several deep breaths, imagining that she was pushing the air down into the pit of her stomach. It was a yogic relaxation technique she'd learned from an old boyfriend. It seemed to help somehow. Her eyes roamed the dingy kitchen. She'd have to be careful, he was her only hope, her ticket out of this dump. She lit a cigarette and exhaled sharply. She sat smoking in the gloom for a considerable period of time. Eventually she picked up the phone and dialed mechanically. She fidgeted while the urgent double ring continued for several seconds. Then someone answered.

CHAPTER 10

The next morning, while ducking out of the Wrecker's Rest en route to the teahouse, Powell and Black had been confronted by a surly Mrs. Polfrock who demanded to know if they would be staying the full two weeks after all. Powell informed her in his most officious manner that they were in Penrick at the pleasure of the local constabulary, and that she might wish to check with Chief Inspector Butts. It occurred to him at the time that he hadn't run into Mr. Polfrock for a while, except for the odd glimpse of him scurrying furtively in the background.

After a brief conference with Sergeant Black over a croissant and coffee, Powell drove to St. Ives to meet with Chief Inspector Butts, listening to disposable pop on Radio One. Once a thriving fishing port, St. Ives was now known as a tourist center and artists' colony, although it had been said by one wag that all the artists of any renown were either dead or had long since fled. The extent to which the bohemian spirit of the place had withered was epitomized in a recent letter sent by the St. Ives Town Council to the Chamber of Commerce asking its

119

members to stop displaying saucy postcards outside their shops. Apparently the councillors hold the view that the reputation of St. Ives as an artists' center will be damaged if visitors on their way to the art galleries are confronted by traditional seaside pictures of seminude women. It wasn't difficult to imagine more than one now-respectable artist of the St. Ives school, whose work was considered scandalous in its day, spinning in his or her grave.

For all that, St. Ives retains an undeniable charm with its narrow streets and picturesque harbor, sandy beaches, and well-kept houses clinging to the hills that climb around the bay. At this time of year traffic was light, and Powell located the police station without difficulty.

Chief Inspector Butts did not exactly look thrilled to see him. "Good morning, Mr. Powell. The fax you were expecting just arrived from London a few minutes ago. The one from the coastguard came in last night."

"Let's have a look at them."

Butts handed the papers over. A list of women reported missing in the past month compiled by one of Powell's colleagues at the Yard and a report from the Coastguard Operations Centre in Falmouth in connection with the recent boating mishap in the English Channel off Torquay. Powell skimmed through the list of missing persons and then turned his attention to the coastguard report.

It seemed that on the evening of April 15, a party of four—two men and two women—had set out from Torquay for a joyride in a sixteen-foot motor launch. The launch was reported by several witnesses to be traveling at a high rate of speed and swerving from side to side in a reckless manner. A small dinghy operated by a local fisherman was nearly swamped in the speedboat's wake. It was subsequently reported by one observer that just before dark, whilst attempting a sharp turn at high speed, the launch struck a wave broadside and flipped over. All four occupants, who were wearing life jackets, were thrown clear. The two men and one of the women were able to make it back to their capsized boat. Unfortunately, due to strong currents, the other woman was swept out to sea. The three survivors, suffering from hypothermia, were eventually picked up by the local lifeboat crew. Alcohol was considered to be a contributing factor in the accident. The woman still missing was presumed drowned. Her name was Katherine Reynolds, age thirty, five feet three inches tall, brown hair and hazel eyes.

Powell handed the reports back. "Looks promising, don't you think?"

Butts shrugged. "It seems to fit, all right."

Powell leaned back in his chair. "How far would you say it is from Torquay to Penrick—as the fish swims, so to speak?"

Butts thought about it for a moment. "I'd have to check the map to be sure, but off the top of my head I'd say it's got to be one hundred fifty miles, give or take."

"According to the coastguard officer I spoke to, the average current speed in these waters is about two knots. To allow for the vagaries of wind and tide and so on, let's assume an average speed of drift of one knot. Let's see, one hundred fifty miles divided by twenty-four miles a day . . . I make it about six days, say a week to be on the safe side."

Butts seemed to be getting into the spirit of things.

"That sounds about right, assuming the body didn't get caught up somewhere."

"That's a good point. But let's keep it simple for present purposes. Do you have a calendar handy?"

Butts reached into his jacket pocket for his appointment book and handed it to Powell.

"Let's see, the accident is reported to have occurred on Tuesday, April fifteenth. The Riddle was first reported in Penrick the following Monday, that would be April twenty-first; so far, so good. Our body was recovered on the Sands two weeks later on Monday, May fifth. What's today—the tenth?" Powell paused for a moment to collect his thoughts. "Sir Reggie conducted the postmortem the day before yesterday—that would be the eighth," he continued. "He indicated that the most likely time of death was fourteen to sixteen days earlier." Powell digressed for a few minutes and summarized Sir Reggie's findings.

"That's bloody peculiar," Butts muttered.

"That would put it somewhere between the twenty-second and twenty-fourth of April, about a week after our accident in Torquay and around the time the Riddle was first reported in Penrick," Powell said.

Butts frowned. "It doesn't seem to fit, then."

"I think it might be close enough—Sir Reggie has indicated that there is considerable uncertainty in this case—but a positive ID would help."

"Light at the end of the tunnel, sir?"

"Not quite. We may have explained where the body came from, but not what was subsequently done to it."

"Probably just some hooligans out to make trouble," Butts said unconvincingly.

Powell examined his colleague critically. "You don't really believe that, do you?"

"What's your theory?" Butts asked defensively.

"Think about the logistics involved to pull the thing off. Whoever is responsible has gone to a lot of trouble to make their point."

"Which is?"

"I was hoping you could tell me."

Butts folded his hands and placed them carefully on his desk. He did not speak for several seconds. When he did, his voice was flat, expressionless. "You know about it, don't you?"

"About Ruth Trevenney, you mean?"

Butts nodded wearily.

"Only the bare bones. I know she was murdered near Penrick in the late Sixties and that her body washed up on the Sands under circumstances that bear an uncanny similarity to the Riddle."

"Similar in what way?" Butts did not meet his eye.

"The body of a young woman discovered by a hippie tripping on acid, and a latter-day version that glows in the dark like an hallucination. It's too much of a coincidence. I think you see it, and I think others do as well. Dr. Harris, for instance."

Butts sighed. "I tried to convince myself that there couldn't possibly be a connection. Then I asked myself, Why would they bring in the Yard for a routine investigation? I realized then that there must be something to it." He looked at Powell. "It was a terrible thing, sir. It was nineteen-sixty-seven. I'd just joined up and was posted in St. Agnes. It was the first murder I'd ever come close to. I wasn't directly involved—not in an official capacity, I mean—but I grew up in Penrick and knew Ruth. She was a lovely girl, as fresh as a spring day. I fancied her a bit, although she was a few years younger than me. It seemed like such a senseless and brutal crime. Her throat cut and then her body thrown into an abandoned mine like a piece of refuse." His expression darkened. "And there's more. There was evidence that she'd been, er, interfered with."

"You mean raped?"

"Yes."

It occurred to Powell that he only knew of one pervert in Penrick. "Go on."

"There's not much more to tell, really. The police investigation drew a complete blank. The conventional wisdom at the time was that it must have been an outsider, a drifter, one of the hippies from Mawgawan Beach, maybe."

"What do *you* think?"

"I was no different than the rest. I couldn't bring myself to believe anything else. How could it have been one of us?" He paused. "Then your Riddle turned up."

"Any ideas?"

Butts frowned and shook his head. "I wouldn't even know where to start. When it comes right down to it, the whole thing doesn't make much sense, does it? Whoever killed Ruth is probably long gone, or even dead. In any case, who would want to draw attention to it now? Certainly not the murderer."

Exactly, Powell thought. Unless—

"I almost forgot, sir! My lads turned up something in the towans near where you and Ms. Goode found the body. An old cart, like the ones they used to use to unload the fish from the boats. You still see a few of 'em around. I'm having forensics go over it with a fine-tooth comb. It occurred to me that it could have been used to haul a body around, but I didn't want to say anything until I was sure." A surprised look from Powell. "I suppose I should have mentioned it earlier, but I took the liberty, that is I thought . . ."

Powell smiled. "Never apologize for showing initiative, Butts." He was beginning to change his opinion about Buttie, who couldn't after all do anything about the fact that Agnes Polfrock was his sister-in-law. "Did you find anything else?"

Butts grimaced. "A number of condoms, from last summer, no doubt—it's too bloody cold this time of year—a pair of tights stuffed down a rabbit hole, empty beer and wine bottles, that's about it."

"That reminds me of something I've been meaning to ask you: Do you chaps deal much with smuggling these days?"

Butts shrugged. "Customs deals with the occasional drug haul, mostly cannabis and cocaine. The stuff generally comes over from North Africa via Spain or Gibraltar by yacht, then it's loaded onto smaller fishing boats, or the like, and landed at any one of a hundred secluded coves up and down the coast."

"What about liquor?"

"As I'm sure you know, sir," Butts said diplomatically, "there's a lot of illegal importation of liquor, but it's pretty hard to keep tabs on."

Chalk up another point for Buttie. "And pornography?"

Butts raised an eyebrow. "Well, sir, you can get pretty

well anything you want in this country nowadays, so I don't see much point."

Unless one doesn't get out much, Powell thought. "Right, then. I'll fax the coastguard report off to Sir Reggie for him to ruminate on, and you can let me know if you learn anything more about that cart. In the meantime, Black and I will do a bit more poking around in Penrick. But unless something develops in the next little while, I'm afraid the Riddle is likely to remain just that." Powell got to his feet. "Oh, and thanks for your help."

Butts escorted Powell to the door of his office. He smiled ruefully. "We didn't get off to a very good start, did we, sir? I was more concerned about my turf than the business at hand."

"If the tables were turned I'd feel the same way at first," Powell said generously. But it did occur to him that Buttie had perhaps gone beyond the pale in one particular respect. "Oh, by the way," he remarked offhandedly, "I'm afraid that Sergeant Black and I have upset your sister-in-law by taking our meals elsewhere."

Butts was suddenly white-faced. "I only sent you there to keep peace in the family. Good God—I hope you don't think I meant it *personally*!"

Powell suppressed a self-satisfied smile, confident that a penitent Buttie would soon set things right at the Wrecker's Rest.

CHAPTER 11

Sergeant Black walked along the beach path toward Towey Head, taking the morning air and rather enjoying himself. With his superior away in St. Ives, he'd taken the opportunity to do a little exploring on his own. Not that he didn't usually feel free to follow his nose whenever the urge struck him; it was just that, well, Mr. Powell had his ways and he had his. He searched his mind for an analogy. Mr. Powell could perhaps be described as a setter, flashy and stylish, at his best in pursuit of a skittish covey of grouse. Black considered himself more of a bloodhound, steady and thorough, from which no furry villain was safe, however deep it went to ground. They made a good team in his estimation, the one's style complementing the other's. For all that, he felt the need to strike off on his own from time to time, to follow his instincts—where his methods wouldn't be subjected to impatient scrutiny by his mercurial superior.

He took a deep breath, then spoke expressively,

"The dusky night rides down the sky,
And ushers in the morn;
The hounds all join in glorious cry,
The huntsman winds his horn:
And a-hunting we will go."

Books illuminated life, right enough, just like his English Lit. teacher had said. Before signing up for that first evening class, he reckoned he'd been wandering through the world like a man missing one of his senses. The great works of literature opened up a whole new universe that had hitherto been denied him. He'd never had the opportunity to get a good education like Mr. Powell, not that he was one to complain about his lot in life. You just had to get on with it and do the best you could with what you had. And although he wasn't particularly competitive by nature, he had to admit a certain feeling of satisfaction now that Mr. Powell had taken notice of his newly acquired literary knowledge.

He paused to take in the view. A large flat rock beside the path provided a convenient seat. He unwrapped the ham sandwich the lady at the teahouse had kindly packed for him at breakfast and was pleased to see she'd included an extra dill pickle. He munched away happily. It was another fine morning. The tide was coming in with long rollers breaking on the Sands. Off to his left was the maze of sand dunes they called the towans. A bloke could wander in there and never come out, he thought. Just opposite was the spot where Ms. Goode had found the body, and up ahead was the little cluster of cottages at the base of Towey Head. He'd never been beyond this point.

This is more like it, he thought. Nothing like a bit of

sea air to clear the mind. He'd spent a hectic day yesterday tracking down the remaining witnesses who had reported seeing the Riddle. He'd managed to talk to all of them except one bloke who was out of town for a few days. It was a curious thing. Although the various accounts differed in a number of details, as one might expect, there did seem to be a common theme running through most of them: someone out for an evening stroll along the Sands, a grotesque object spotted at the water's edge, usually, although not always, emanating a weird greenish light, and the witness not bothering to stay around for a closer look. And strangest of all, the Riddle seemed to pop out of sight as suddenly as it appeared. On more than one occasion, individuals reported returning to the scene ten or fifteen minutes later with reinforcements to corroborate the sighting only to find that the damn thing had disappeared. To pull off something like that would take a bit of fancy footwork. But at this point the *how* was less important to him than the *why*. He had a few ideas but needed to work the thing through a bit more.

He finished the last of his sandwich, folded the grease paper neatly, and put it in his jacket pocket. Then he got stiffly to his feet. Time to check out the neighborhood.

A half dozen cottages, all except two boarded up for the season. A freshly painted bungalow with a flower garden in full bloom (Dr. Harris's cottage, of course) sat next door to a rather run-down stone-built affair with a cluttered front garden that he reckoned must be the Porters'. There was no sign of life at Dr. Harris's, nor any sign of his black Vauxhall in the back.

Black was standing in front of the doctor's cottage

debating what to do next when a movement behind the Porters' caught his eye. Someone was hightailing it up the path behind the cottage. He had an impression of a tall bloke with an awkward gait. In an instant the man disappeared into the lane, obscured by the tall hedgerow. Black had been about to call after him, but something stopped him. He wasn't sure if the man had seen him. He scratched his balding head. It seemed a bit odd, so he decided that he'd better investigate on the off chance there was some funny business going on.

He moved stealthily between the two cottages, taking to the lawn on Dr. Harris's property rather than the brick walk on the Porters' side. He stopped and looked around the back of the small stone house. Nothing out of the ordinary. He walked up to the back door and peered through the window. It was too dark inside to see much of anything, just a puddle of light here and there beneath a tiny window.

He cocked an ear. Had he heard something just then? For just an instant he could have sworn he'd heard the sound of voices coming from the far side of the cottage. He inched along the back wall, listened for a moment, and then poked his head around the corner. There was only the murmuring of the sea. Perhaps he'd been mistaken. The Porters' was the last in the row of cottages, and only a short stretch of rough foreshore littered with some rusting machinery and an old wooden skiff separated it from the base of Towey Head. Black looked up at the summit of the dark prominence; it certainly looked foreboding from this vantage point, like a stern judge, towering in his black robes above the dock, passing judgment on those below. Nice simile for the human condition, that—

There it was again! More distinct now, coming from a small window in the side of the cottage. A woman's voice, inarticulate, and then a sort of whimpering sound, punctuated by a deeper voice, guttural and slightly muffled. Now the telltale creaking of bedsprings. Blushing profusely, Black beat a hasty retreat; he didn't pause to catch his breath until he was standing once again in front of Dr. Harris's cottage.

He knew it was silly to feel embarrassed, but he had a thing about Peeping Toms. He had no doubt interrupted Mr. and Mrs. Porter while they were engaged in marital relations, and he knew how he would feel if the shoe were on the other foot. He scratched his head. Still, that bloke ducking up the back lane was a rum business. He mulled over the various possibilities. As he started back for Penrick, he decided he had better mention it to Mr. Powell.

That afternoon while Powell and Sergeant Black sat in the Head comparing notes, Nick Tebble worked in the machine shed behind the Old Fish Cellar. Ostensibly, the object of his attention was the rusty and decrepit motor that in the old days had powered the winch used to hoist the fish up from the boats. In actual fact he would have been unable to say exactly what he was doing or why he was doing it. Aimless pottering was a kind of defense mechanism he had developed over the years to avoid thinking about things. But this time it didn't seem to be helping. Too much had happened, and he felt like he was about to explode, like the telly in his head had been turned up full blast. He threw down his spanner. He had to think. They were trying to get him, he knew that, to put him away in some deep dark place, just like—his laughter ripping through the silence like shrapnel. They thought they could buy him off, the bastards! Like he didn't know what he was about.

He began arranging his tools as a small boy might array his collection of tin soldiers in anticipation of some ultimate childhood Armageddon. Suddenly he froze. A small sound outside, his eyes narrowing. He moved toward the door to investigate. There was a silent figure silhouetted against the dazzling sunlight.

Tebble blinked for a few seconds and then recognition flickered on his face. He sneered. "I been thinkin' about tha'—"

It seemed to be happening in slow motion, the spade ripping into his abdomen muscles tearing blood searing hot and gushing his trousers soaked pooling on the ground and slippery on his hands as he grasped the wooden handle tightly like he did when he was a boy and his father pulled him over the snow sitting on this spade behind their horse, his hands not cold now but warm and sticky as the handle was pulled from his grasp. Dad? He looked up, bewildered, an instant before the blade caught him on the side of the head and crushed his skull.

The message was delivered to Powell and Black at ten past four. When they arrived at the Old Fish Cellar fifteen minutes later, an Incident Van was already parked behind the gray stone house, blocking the drive. They walked down the steep incline toward an old wooden shed standing between the house and a straggling garden, where most of the activity seemed to be concentrated. Scene-of-crime officers bustled purposefully about, and it didn't take the detectives long to locate Chief Inspector Butts.

Butts grimaced. "I hope you chaps haven't had your tea." He led the way to the door of the shed, where a police photographer was focusing on an object lying on the ground just to the right of the doorway. The lower half of a supine human torso protruded from the shed.

Powell forced himself to examine the object of the photographer's attention first. It was a long-handled Cornish spade, of the type used for digging potatoes. The blade and the lower half of the bleached wooden handle were liberally coated with blood.

He then turned his attention to the shed's doorway. There was blood everywhere: a thickening red puddle debouching like a viscous river from the interior; the boots and trousers stained dark; the faded planks surrounding the doorway splattered up to a height of about seven feet.

He looked back down at the body. The greasy shirt was sliced open at the midriff. There was a dark crescent-shaped wound just below the navel, leering like some gory smile. And the familiar cloying smell of death.

"He's still warm," Butts commented.

Powell gestured toward the shed. "May I go inside?"

"Go ahead, sir. I think we've got everything we need."

Powell stepped neatly over the corpse, avoiding most of the gore, and once inside made a quick survey. The interior of the shed was garishly illuminated by a mechanic's light that someone had suspended from one of the rafters. Various bits of machinery, garden tools, rusted engine blocks, and stacks of cardboard boxes leaning precariously along the walls. The smell of grease-soaked rags and fertilizer. On the workbench an ancient engine of some description, partly disassembled. Powell turned back to the body. The right side of the head was severely lacerated and Tebble's eyes were wide and staring. The abdominal wound looked like a frown from this vantage point.

Powell stepped back into the fresh air. "Well, what do you think?"

Butts frowned. "It doesn't take a genius to figure out what happened. Somebody skewered him with that spade and then caved his head in with it, or possibly the other way around. The police surgeon should be here shortly to sort it out." He shook his head slowly. "It's the *why* that's got me puzzled. Nick Tebble was a bit odd, from what I knew of him, but I've always considered him basically harmless. The sort of chap who minded his own business."

"Any run-ins with the law?" Powell asked.

Butts shrugged. "His family has lived here for generations, and there's never been any trouble, as far as I know."

"Who reported it?"

"The postman delivering the afternoon mail."

Powell nodded. "Any sign of visitors?"

"Not as far as we can tell, but we're still looking. There're marks all over the place, as you might expect, probably Tebble's. Whoever wielded the spade was evidently wearing gloves. There's an assortment of boot prints along the drive where it's damp, but as you can see, sir, the ground around the shed here is quite hard packed."

"Any sign of a disturbance in the house?"

"Nothing obvious, sir. But it's pretty chaotic in there. Housekeeping obviously wasn't his speciality."

Powell grunted. "Well, Butts, you seem to have things well in hand."

Butts looked puzzled. "I assumed you'd be taking charge, sir."

Powell smiled reassuringly. "Now, why would you assume that? But if you don't mind, I'd like to have a quick look around the grounds with Sergeant Black before we go."

Butts looked relieved. "Of course, sir."

Powell and Black walked around to the front of the house and stood at the top of the stone wall that separated the front garden from the beach. There were the rusted remnants of a winch at the top of the wall, which Powell surmised had once been used to haul up the fish. A narrow set of steps descended steeply to the beach. The tide was flooding and the sea lapped at the shingle a few feet from the base of the wall. A small wooden skiff, which was attached by means of a long painter to an iron ring fixed to the wall, drifted aimlessly back and forth. A hundred feet away, the surf crashed against the rocks that guarded the entrance to the little cove.

Powell looked back at the Old Fish Cellar. A large herring gull was perched motionless on the roof, silhouetted against the granite-colored sky. Sergeant Black scratched his head in that characteristic manner of his.

"Well, Bill, what do you make of it?"

Black considered his superior's question carefully before answering. "I'm thinking about Tebble's set-to with Tony Rowlands in the Head the other night, sir."

Powell did not get the opportunity to reply. There was

a commotion around the back of the house and, an instant later, Chief Inspector Butts was hurrying over. His face was taut. "I guess you *will* be taking charge, after all, sir."

"What do you mean?"

"One of my men was poking around in the cellar. There was a barrel down there, Mr. Powell, and . . ." He hesitated.

"Yes, Butts, what is it?"

"In the barrel, sir." He swallowed hard. "A hand. A human hand. And it's wearing a bloody engagement ring!"

CHAPTER 12

"You mean he *pickled* her?" Jane Goode was incredulous. "I don't believe it!"

Powell drained his pint with a gulp. "Well, *somebody's* left hand was found packed in salt at the Old Fish Cellar, and I'm willing to bet my pension that it belongs to your Riddle. And furthermore, I'll wager you a drink that Tebble's woodpile glows in the dark."

She smiled wanly. "I never gamble. But I wonder what it all means?"

"It explains why the body was so well preserved, for one thing. I can hardly wait to tell Sir Reggie about this; it'll make his day. And while we're on the subject of preservatives, I need another pint. More wine?"

She nodded.

Tony Rowlands was nowhere in evidence that evening, but Powell managed to attract the barmaid's attention.

Jenny Thompson's face was pale as she delivered the drinks. "I still can't get over Nick Tebble," she volunteered. "It's just awful."

"Very sad," Powell agreed. "Is Tony around?" Casual, like.

She shook her head irritably. "He was in earlier. It's getting busy—I could use a hand."

When she'd gone, Powell lit a cigarette.

"That's a disgusting habit."

"I have worse."

They sat in silence for a few moments, each preoccupied with his or her own thoughts.

Eventually Powell spoke, "What were you saying before?"

"What? Oh, I was just trying to make sense of it all."

He exhaled slowly. "I think it's pretty clear what happened. The body of our missing boater from Torquay washes up on the beach near the Old Fish Cellar one day. For whatever reason, Tebble seizes the opportunity and concocts the Riddle, or perhaps I should say 'Ruse' of Penrick. A liberal sprinkling of luminous fungus scraped from some rotting log for effect, and some fairly intricate maneuvering to stage the thing, which explains why the Riddle was only seen at night. During the day he kept the corpse preserved in brine in his cellar. It all fits."

Jane shook her head doubtfully. "I still don't see how he pulled it off. Getting it back and forth, for instance, and never getting caught in the act."

"Oh, our Nick was a cagey bugger. He carries the body between the Old Fish Cellar and the Sands in his skiff at night. Then he dumps it on the beach, doctors it up with the fungus, and hides out in the towans where he can keep an eye on things. An unsuspecting passerby out for an evening stroll along the Sands stumbles onto the thing and, not surprisingly, flees for dear life—present company excepted, of course. When the coast is clear, Tebble loads the corpse back in his skiff and heads home for the salt cellar. Buttie's lads found an old cart in the towans that Tebble may have used to move the body around. He could easily have used it to pack his skiff a short distance into the towans as well, which would explain why none of the witnesses ever reported seeing a boat. Brilliant, don't you think?"

Jane Goode smiled crookedly. "You or Tebble?"

"Very funny."

"What went wrong then? Why was the body still there when we went back?"

Powell shrugged. "You remember the storm that night? There was a short piece of frayed rope attached to the life jacket. Tebble probably tied the body to a rock or an anchor of some sort to keep it from getting away from him. The rope must have broke. We'll probably never know for sure."

She took a sip of her wine. "It sounds plausible enough, but you haven't answered the most important question of all."

"You mean the sixty-four thousand dollar question, as our American friends say: Why did he do it?"

She nodded eagerly. "Exactly. Any ideas?"

Powell looked at her with amusement. "What do *you* think?"

She scoffed. "It's obvious, isn't it?"

"Really?"

She glanced around the pub to make sure no one was watching them and then said in a conspiratorial whisper, "Ruth Trevenney is the key, I just know it!"

He was about to say something when, predictably on

cue, Sergeant Black walked through the door and made a beeline for their table.

Powell sighed. "Yes, Black, what is it?"

Black's expression was serious as he sat down. He looked at Jane Goode then back at Powell. Powell nodded almost imperceptibly.

"This afternoon, back at the Old Fish Cellar, sir. Something was bothering me, but I couldn't put my finger on it. It suddenly struck me. It was Tebble's skiff. I'm certain it was the same one I saw pulled up on the beach near the Porters' this morning."

Powell said nothing and stared into his empty glass. The atmosphere had suddenly grown oppressive, as if a storm were brewing.

Jane Goode fidgeted impatiently until she could bear it no longer. "So?"

Powell ignored her. He looked up at Black. *"What men call gallantry, and Gods adultery, is much more common where the climate's sultry."*

"My thoughts exactly, sir."

Powell caught up with Dr. Harris the next morning as he was returning home from church, which perhaps explained the old man's philosophical turn of mind. He had obviously heard about the murder.

"Whatever else we may like to think, Chief Superintendent, it is death that defines the human condition. My own profession is no more than a charade, a well-intentioned but ultimately futile attempt to delay the inevitable. False hopes are a doctor's truck and trade; we're really no better than witch doctors in that respect. If you take away the advances made in reducing infant mortality in the past century, medical science has done very little to extend the human life span beyond our allotted fourscore and ten." He shook his head sadly. "And the tragedy is that most of us fritter away our lives in pursuit of meaningless gratification."

Powell nodded neutrally. "Did you know Nick Trebble?" he asked quietly.

"Not really. I'd see him from time to time in the village. He was always rowing back and forth in that little boat of his."

"I understand he was a bit of a loner."

Harris sighed. "We're all very much alone in this world, each in our own way. But I think that's true. The only time I can recall seeing him in what one might call a social situation was in the Head, but even there he usually sat by himself."

"He must have had *some* friends or associates. Did you ever see him over at the Porters', for instance?" Powell persisted.

Harris gave him a circumspect look. "Not that I can recall."

"I hope you don't mind answering all these questions."

A paper-thin smile. "Not at all, Chief Superintendent; it makes me feel useful. But there must be a point to it."

"There is, actually, now that you mention it. I need to know about Roger Trevenney."

An awkward silence.

Eventually Harris spoke. "What do you want to know?"

"Everything, starting with his daughter."

Harris sighed heavily. "I see." He then went on to relate the story of Ruth's murder, how she just disappeared one afternoon, the macabre circumstances in which her body was found, the fruitless murder investigation that followed, and finally the impact the tragedy had on the village. And then some thirty years later, the resurrection of painful memories by the Riddle, with its crude and rather obvious implications.

The account was essentially similar to the others Powell had heard, until Harris got around to the subject of Roger Trevenney himself.

"Roger was a wonderful artist, as you've seen yourself. Still is, come to that, although he hasn't painted much in recent years."

Powell's attention was drawn once again to Trevenney's painting in the little alcove in Dr. Harris's sitting room. He walked over and searched the impressionistic seascape for hidden clues.

"You see, Ruth's death took it out of him," Dr. Harris was saying. "He'd lost his wife some years before, and Ruth was everything to him." He looked at Powell with watery eyes. "I can understand how he must have felt. He told me years later that he seriously contemplated suicide. It was only the thought of what Ruth would have wanted that deterred him." Dr. Harris suddenly looked very frail. "And there was something else . . ." He hesitated. "I think Roger was determined to discover the identity of his daughter's murderer."

This caught Powell's attention. "What gave you that idea?"

"Roger is basically an optimist, which is rather amazing considering what he's been through. In a way, I think the thought that Ruth's murderer might eventually be brought to justice has kept him going."

"I'm getting the impression that you know him quite well."

"I've been his physician for years. After my Helen died, Roger and I became close friends, two widowers seeking companionship, I suppose."

Powell nodded understandingly. "When I first came to see you, you mentioned that Roger was not very well. What did you mean?"

"He has an inoperable brain tumor. *Glioblastoma multiforme* is the medical term for it. At best, he has only a few months to live. He has his ups and downs, but as you can imagine, this ghastly business has taken its toll. I looked in on him yesterday morning and he seemed very weak."

Powell didn't know what to say. "I'm sorry."

Harris grew philosophical again. "Ah, well, Chief Superintendent, the human condition, remember?" A lengthy silence. "There's something about this place that seeps into your soul," he said eventually. "The barrows and mounds and stone circles that mark the ancient graves." He looked at Powell. "Death, like the sea, is ever present."

Powell was troubled by Dr. Harris's morbid tone. He spoke carefully. "I'm going to have to talk to Mr. Trevenney."

Harris stared at him, uncomprehending.

"It's Tebble, you see," Powell said gently, "I didn't mention it before, but it appears that the Riddle was *his* doing, and that's probably why he was killed."

CHAPTER 13

Powell decided to pay a visit to the Head alone. Sergeant Black was off running some errands, and Jane had secluded herself in her room to write. Another newspaper story, Powell wondered, or was she finally getting down to work on her novel? He arrived at the pub before noon hoping to have a quiet word with Tony Rowlands. Except for the publican, the bar was empty.

"Chief Superintendent. Long time, no see." He slurred his words slightly; he had obviously been drinking.

"Hello, Tony. How goes the battle?"

"Can't complain. Even if I did, no one would listen. Ha ha!"

A false note sounded in Powell's mind. "Terrible thing about Nick Tebble . . ."

The smile never left Rowlands's face, but his eyes were brittle. "Yeah, well, he was a bit of a nutter, that one."

"I beg your pardon?" Powell kept his voice even.

"I mean he was a bit strange, wasn't he? What he did to that body—it makes my skin crawl."

144

The word had obviously got out. "But I wonder why somebody would want to disembowel him with a spade," Powell mused.

Rowlands shrugged. "Beats me. Transients, maybe? I heard there was some kids camping down at Mawgawan Beach."

Powell stared at Rowlands. "Why do you suppose he did it?"

"What?"

"The Riddle."

"Oh, that. Like I said, he was bonkers. Didn't like tourists, for one thing. If you want my opinion, I think he did it to scare people off."

Powell affected an air of puzzlement. "It had the opposite effect, surely."

"What do you mean?"

"The newspaper stories, the notoriety; I even saw a sign in a shop window the other day: *Home of the Riddle of Penrick.*"

Rowlands a bit edgy now. "Well, like I said, Nick wasn't exactly an intellectual giant. Now, if you don't mind, Chief Superintendent, I should be getting on with—"

Powell was undeterred. "Knew him well, did you?"

An impatient sigh. "Not well, no."

"You've been in Penrick—how long now?—some thirty-odd years?"

"That's right."

"I imagine old Nick was one of your regular customers."

"He came in for a drink now and then."

"By the way, do you happen to know how old he was?"

"Early fifties, I would imagine. Does it matter?"

"He was in here the other night, as I recall."

Rowlands's expression tightened. "What of it?"

"You were having a disagreement about something."

"It wasn't important." An attempt to sound casual.

Powell looked at him mildly. "Oh? I seem to remember you telling him you'd break his bloody neck, or words to that effect."

"What are you driving at?" Rowlands blurted out.

"That's what you said."

"Well, I mean, he'd had too much too drink, hadn't he? So I cut him off. When he made a fuss, I asked him to leave. That's all there was to it."

Powell didn't believe a word of it. "I have to ask you about your whereabouts yesterday afternoon, Tony."

Rowlands shook his head in disbelief. "I was here serving you and Sergeant Black when he was killed."

Powell let the silence stretch out. Eventually he spoke. "How do you know when he was killed?"

Rowlands flushed. "I don't know . . . I just assumed . . ."

Powell drained his pint, letting him stew. "Thanks, Tony, I must be off. We can continue this little chat later."

Powell drove south along the coastal road, preoccupied with his thoughts. At intervals narrow hedge-enclosed lanes branched off to the west, descending by way of steep, narrow valleys toward the sea. He'd already passed the turning to Dr. Harris's and the Porters', and the one to the Old Fish Cellar; he was looking for the track that led eventually to Roger Trevenney's house. The sea and sky were a dull gunmetal gray and a light mist hung in the air. The landscape was reduced to a wash of pastel colors in the flat light; drab green fields crisscrossed with the ubiquitous gray stone walls, and here and there an occasional sad cow. Off to his right loomed the dark shape of an engine house, the stone and brick chimney jutting into the sky like a medieval keep. He wondered if it marked the location of the old mine workings where Ruth Trevenney's body had been hidden.

It seemed to Powell, as he negotiated the bumps and potholes, that the murder of Nick Tebble and the gruesome discovery at the Old Fish Cellar only provided further tantalizing clues to the tragic events of thirty years ago. From what he knew, Tebble didn't strike him as the type of individual who would perpetrate an elaborate hoax like the Riddle for a lark. He was convinced now that the intent had been deadly serious. Serious enough for Tebble to have got himself killed. He wondered how old Tebble would have been when Ruth was murdered—twenty-one or twenty-two? Perhaps he'd been sweet on Ruth. Maybe he had some idea who killed her, and the Riddle was his attempt to flush out the quarry. But if that was the case, why not go to the police?And was it likely that the murderer of Ruth Trevenney would have remained in Penrick all these years? Somebody forty years old at the time would be over seventy now.

And what about Tony Rowlands, the not-so-jolly publican, who gets into a very public altercation with the victim less than a week before the murder? Most intriguing of all was the possibility that Black had caught Tebble and Linda Porter in flagrante delicto a few hours before Tebble was murdered. The fact that his skiff was pulled up on the beach near the Porters' cottage was certainly suggestive, as was Black's description of the man he saw running up the back lane, who sounded suspiciously like Jim Porter. Powell frowned. Too many questions and not enough answers.

The terrain became rougher, pastureland gradually giving way to bracken and boulders with thickets of blackthorn, brambles, and sharp-pricked gorse. And there, just ahead, a narrow lane swinging off to the right toward the sea cliffs. He descended into the thickening fog. He passed a scattering of outbuildings, ghostly shapes in the mist, and eventually, at the foot of the hill, he could see the outline of a house. He parked his car and got out, the roar of the sea below, and experienced a sense of excited anticipation. It was as if this moment had been preordained.

He was greeted at the door by a tall, slightly stooping man with pale, sharp features and thin white hair. The man smiled wanly. "Mr. Powell, I presume. Please come in. I hope my directions were clear."

"Perfectly clear, Mr. Trevenney."

They shook hands.

"It's a pleasure to meet you, sir," Powell said. "I've admired your painting at Dr. Harris's."

Trevenney smiled modestly. "You're most kind, but I haven't done anything that good for years. Here, come into the front room and sit down. I'll get us some tea." Trevenney, a little unstable on his feet, placed his hand momentarily against the wall.

Powell protested, "You needn't trouble yourself—"

"Nonsense! I'll be right back."

Powell made himself at home and took in his surroundings. Despite the gloom outside, the little cottage was bright and cheery. A woman's touch, he would have thought if he hadn't known better: chintz curtains on the windows, a vase of cut flowers on the coffee table, and a log fire crackling in the grate. The focal point of the room hung on the wall above the mantelpiece: a portrait of a young girl in a white dress kneeling in a meadow bright with wildflowers, an impression of massive rocks and a translucent sea as a backdrop. The style was undoubtedly Trevenney's, and the emotional presence of the girl in the painting was almost palpable. She seemed to be look- ing directly at him, her eyes slightly puzzled. He didn't notice Roger Trevenney entering the room.

"My daughter, Ruth," Trevenney said quietly.

"She's very beautiful."

"Yes, she was." It was stated simply, as a matter of fact, without a hint of sadness. He placed the tea things on the coffee table. "I'm sorry I can only offer you a few biscuits. I don't get out to the shops much these days."

"Shortbread is my weakness, Mr. Trevenney."

After pouring the tea and settling himself, Trevenney took a moment to catch his breath. He regarded Powell with apparent interest. "Peter has told me all about you, Chief Superintendent."

"Peter?"

"My old friend Dr. Harris. He keeps me up-to-date with what's happening in the world."

Powell smiled. "What's he been telling you, then?"

"I know that he's told you about my illness. I wanted to let you know that I'm having one of my better days, so you needn't concern yourself with that. I'd much rather you were completely frank with me. Agreed?"

"Yes, of course, sir." Powell experienced a sense of relief. Acutely aware of his own mortality, he had never been much good at dealing with such matters, but his host's candor put him at ease.

Trevenney went on to describe the futile courses of chemotherapy and radiation treatments and the emotional roller-coaster ride that is a cancer patient's life. Finally, he had arrived at the point where he was content to let nature take its course. He spoke in a detached, matter-of-fact manner, and Powell was struck by the quiet dignity of the man.

"Now, Chief Superintendent, I trust with that out of the way we'll be able to concentrate on the business at hand," Trevenney concluded.

"I'll try to be brief, sir. Can I assume that Dr. Harris has told you something about my reasons for coming to see you?"

Trevenney raised an eyebrow. "You want to know how much I know, is that it?"

Powell smiled. "Something like that."

With a trembling hand Trevenney took a sip of his tea. "I know why you came to Penrick. And now, of course, there's that business out at the Old Fish Cellar . . ." He left it hanging.

Powell looked up again at the portrait of the girl hanging on the wall behind Trevenney. He searched her eyes for inspiration.

It was as if Trevenney read his mind. "Over the years I've come to accept what happened to Ruth, Chief Superintendent. I can't say that talking about it isn't difficult for me, but now that my innings are almost up, I want only to see justice done before I finally join my wife and daughter."

"We have a common purpose, then, Mr. Trevenney,"

Powell said. Finishing his tea, he took a moment to collect his thoughts. There was no point in going all round the houses; he had already decided that he could be forthright with the old man. "Nick Tebble is obviously the key to this thing," he began. "Why did he go to so much trouble to stage what appears to be, for all intents and purposes, a reenactment of the discovery of your daughter's body thirty years ago? There are at least two obvious possibilities. It has been suggested to me that Tebble was a bit of an oddball who didn't much like outsiders and who may have conceived the Riddle as a way to scare off tourists and the like. By resurrecting the specter of a previous unsolved murder, he may have been trying to create the impression that the murderer was still abroad." He paused.

"And the second possibility, Chief Superintendent?" Trevenney prompted.

Powell considered his words carefully before replying. "The second possibility is that Tebble knew the identity of Ruth's murderer and was attempting to blackmail that person."

Trevenney drew a shallow breath as if about to say something, but then he seemed to lose track of his thoughts. He looked slightly confused.

The room had grown very dark. Powell glanced out the window. The fog seemed impenetrable now, a suitable metaphor, he thought, for his present state of mind. He wondered what Trevenney had been about to say.

Trevenney reached up and turned on the lamp that stood beside his chair. "Looks like we're in for a spell of nasty weather," he observed.

CHAPTER 14

"She was quite a naturalist, my Ruth. She used to spend hours exploring the countryside. Very observant, she was; she'd write things down in her diary and make sketches of the wildlife and flowers she'd seen. Her drawings of birds were particularly good." Trevenney's eyes had a faraway look, as if he were searching some inner horizon for a ship that was long overdue. "It was a few days after her sixteenth birthday. She set out late one afternoon to visit a secluded megalith that we'd discovered some months previously. It's about a mile from here, up in the hills just before the turning to the cottage. She asked me to go with her, but I was working on a commission at the time and . . ." He hesitated, eyes moist.

"She hadn't returned by evening and naturally I began to fret. When it got dark and there was still no sign of her, I was literally beside myself. I rang the police, but they said they couldn't do anything until morning. A search party was mounted the next day, but there was no trace of her. I combed the hills myself, searching and calling her name . . ." For a moment he seemed unable to continue.

"Then it began to rain," he said. "Three days after she'd disappeared, her body washed up on the Sands. They eventually found some of her clothes at the old mine workings you passed on your way here. She'd been . . ." He left the rest unsaid. "You understand about the tunnel?"

Powell nodded.

Trevenney rubbed his temples with the fingers of both hands.

"Are you feeling all right, sir?" Powell asked.

"Yes, of course," Trevenney said, sounding slightly irritated. "Where was I? Oh, yes. After her body was found, the story was splashed all over the newspapers. It was a very difficult time for me, as you can imagine, but strange as it may sound, what bothered me the most after I'd accepted the reality of Ruth's death was how quickly the police seemed to give up the chase. Perhaps that seems a bit unfair—I realize they didn't have much to go on—but I feel that the very fact you're here, Chief Superintendent, is a kind of vindication."

"I understand perfectly. But tell me, sir, from your own perspective, do you have any theories about what might have happened to your daughter?"

Trevenney considered the question carefully before replying. "I wish I could say that I had. To be frank, I couldn't conceive of anyone wanting to—to hurt her. She was such a kind and gentle person, Mr. Powell. I suppose I've always imagined it must have been a stranger, someone who didn't know her."

Powell thought about all the kind and gentle people in the world who were killed every day by people who knew them. But he had reviewed the file and had come to the same conclusion as Trevenney; it appeared that the police had indeed had very little to go on. "I'm wondering about Nick Tebble," he said. "Do you remember if he lived around here at the time?"

Trevenney frowned. "I don't really remember him—he would have been older than Ruth—but then my memory isn't what it used to be. I knew his father slightly; the family has lived at the Old Fish Cellar for generations."

"You don't remember much about him, then? Whether he knew your daughter, for instance?"

"I wish I could be more helpful, but I'm sorry I just can't . . ." He seemed to lose his train of thought again.

"Do you have any more recent memories of Tebble?"

Trevenney shrugged. "I'd see him around the village occasionally, but I can't say that I recall ever speaking to him. He did seem rather a peculiar fellow, but to be honest, I've never given him much thought until now."

Time to change tacks, Powell thought. "I was talking to Tony Rowlands at the Head earlier today. Do you know him?"

Trevenney smiled. "I suppose you could say that I'm a former client. I used to pop in from time to time for a glass of wine after doing my shopping in the village, or occasionally with Peter of a Saturday evening. I'm afraid that I'm not up to it these days," he added wistfully.

"You don't happen to remember if Rowlands lived in Penrick when your daughter disappeared?"

Trevenney furrowed his brow in concentration. "Yes—yes, I think he took over the Head a year or two earlier. That's right! I remember he was quoted in the papers at the time about the girl who found Ruth. She'd been at the pub earlier that evening."

Powell nodded. "He does serve a good glass of wine, I'll give him that. Not your usual plonk."

"I'm not much of a connoisseur, Chief Superintendent—Peter's the one for good French wine."

Powell smiled. "I've had the pleasure of sampling Dr. Harris's hospitality." He helped himself to a piece of shortbread. "Speaking of wine, I imagine there's still a bit of smuggling that goes on along this coast."

Trevenney gave Powell a shrewd look. "You're not asking me to implicate my old friend, are you?" He seemed reassured by Powell's innocent expression. "It's a bit of a local tradition, fair-trading—liquor and cigarettes, mostly. Not very important in the grand scheme of things, I shouldn't imagine. And one hears about the odd drug haul. But I trust that the local police would be able to enlighten you further on that score." Trevenney looked very tired.

"I won't take any more of your time, Mr. Trevenney. You've been most helpful, and I promise that I'll let you know the moment there is anything to report." As Powell demolished the last of his biscuit, he remembered something. "There is one more thing. When we were discussing Tebble's possible motives in connection with the Riddle, the possibility that he knew the identity of your daughter's assailant, you seemed about to mention something . . ."

"Oh? What could it have been? I can't imagine . . ." He trailed off into a pensive silence.

"Not to worry. If you think of anything else, you can call me at the Wrecker's Rest." Powell rose to leave. "Please don't get up. I'll see myself out." He hesitated. "Take care, Mr. Trevenney."

Trevenney stared out the window at the fog, his attention miles way. It had begun to drizzle and rivulets of water were streaming down the glass. "What? Oh, yes, yes, of course," he said faintly, a puzzled expression on his face.

Powell got back to the Wrecker's Rest around four o'clock and found Sergeant Black and Chief Inspector Butts conferring in the dining room over a cup of tea. Butts had taken a room in the guesthouse and planned to remain in Penrick for the duration of the investigation.

Powell collapsed wearily into a chair. "Anything to report?" he asked.

"A few interesting tidbits on Nick Tebble, sir," Butts said.

"I'm all ears."

"For starters, he was fifty-two years old—"

"That would make him twenty-two when the Trevenney girl was murdered," Powell interjected.

"Right. Now here's the curious thing. He doesn't seem to have ever worked for a living."

"What do you mean?"

"I mean there isn't any employment history or tax records. Nothing. Not even a driver's license."

Powell frowned. "Perhaps he had a private income."

"If he did, sir, it must have come out of thin air. He didn't even have a bank account, at least not under his own name."

Curious, but then Powell imagined that Tebble would have been more or less self-sufficient out at the Old Fish Cellar—fishing, growing his own vegetables, and what have you. "What about his parents?"

"Both died years ago. And there are no other surviving relatives, as far as we've been able to determine."

"A bit of a mystery man," Sergeant Black observed.

Butts nodded, a troubled expression on his face. "It looks that way. He was about my age, but I never had much to do with him when I was a lad." He looked at Powell hesitantly. "Er, I've taken the liberty of asking Agnes about him, sir . . ." He let it hang.

"Oh?"

Butts cleared his throat awkwardly. "You know what Agnes is like, Mr. Powell—you have to take her with a grain of salt—but I think you should hear what she has to say."

Powell glanced at Black who was grinning broadly. "All right, if you think it would help."

Butts left to fetch Mrs. Polfrock and Powell looked at Black. "What do you think, Bill?" he said.

"I think it's a funny business, Mr. Powell."

Powell sighed. "Any ideas?"

"I'd like to follow up on the smuggling angle; it's been bothering me. A bit of wine here—" he screwed up his face "—some dirty magazines there. It seems like small beer, but I think there's a connection somewhere."

"Why don't you do that. I'm going to—" He was interrupted by Butts, who had returned to their table with a reticent Mrs. Polfrock in tow. Powell stood up. "Mrs. Polfrock, this is indeed an unexpected pleasure. Please sit down."

"Yes, well, anything I can do to help," she said, refusing to meet his eye. She was strangely subdued.

Butts must have laid down the law, Powell thought.

"Buttie tells me that you have something to tell us about Nick Tebble."

A sudden flash of the familiar Mrs. Polfrock. "He was a bad 'un, Mr. Powell. He got what he deserved, if you want my opinion."

"Agnes, really!" Butts protested.

"Interfering with dead bodies like that, and God knows what else! It's perverted!"

A minor clatter in the front hall. Mr. Polfrock fleeing the scene? Powell wondered. "Do you have any idea why he might have done it?" He observed her closely.

"He was a bloody loony," she said dogmatically, as if there could be absolutely no doubt about it.

Powell formulated his next question carefully. "What prior evidence do you have that Nick Tebble was, er, unbalanced?"

"Unbalanced, that's a good one, that is!" She laughed harshly.

Powell waited patiently. He noticed that Butts was fidgeting in his chair.

"Well, they would hardly let him out of the house, would they?" she said.

"Who? His parents?"

"Who else?"

"Would you care to elaborate, Mrs. Polfrock?"

She was obviously unhappy at being pressed for a logical explanation of her beliefs. "I can't explain it. He was never right from the start; that's all I know."

Powell sighed. He had dealt with her type so many times before. "Is there anything else you'd care to add?"

She shook her head stubbornly. "I know you don't believe me, but mark my words, he was a bad 'un."

Later, sitting alone with Sergeant Black, Powell was vaguely ill at ease. What was it Rashid had said in his inimitable fashion that night at the restaurant? Never trust a tiger that changes his spots. One thing was certain: Agnes Polfrock had remained true to character. And oddly enough, he was inclined to believe her.

Black was obviously puzzled at his superior's apparent change of heart about their landlady. "I'm not sure I understand, sir. Are you saying that you think there might be something to what she said about Tebble?"

Powell looked at him. *"Do I contradict myself? Very well then I contradict myself. I am large, I contain multitudes."*

"Sir?"

"The American poet, Walt Whitman." He felt a twinge of guilt; it wasn't likely that Black would have studied him in his evening class.

Black, unfazed, nodded his head knowingly. "Right. *Leaves of Grass*, isn't it, sir? I've been meaning to read it."

Powell looked at him in amazement. "You're one of a kind, Bill, did you know that?"

Black smiled shyly. "That's what the missus is always telling me, sir."

CHAPTER 15

The next morning, after a brief conference over a surprisingly digestible Wrecker's Rest breakfast (Powell felt he owed the gesture to Butts in the interest of promoting family harmony), they each went their separate ways. Given the paucity of information about Tebble's background, Butts was off to oversee a more intensive search of the Old Fish Cellar to make sure they hadn't overlooked anything, and Sergeant Black planned to spend the day poking around Penrick in search of dirty books, as Powell had pointedly put it.

For his part, Powell had originally intended to take the day off. Or, more precisely, to spend it with Jane Goode, reconnoitering the local bays and coves in Dr. Harris's Enterprise. The day, however, had dawned wet and dreary, and in any case she had refused to abandon her writing (she was on a roll, apparently) and Powell, feeling slightly put out, was at loose ends. He felt a bit guilty about letting the side down, but he was at the point in the investigation where he felt he needed to get above the mental clouds for a while. He drove off in the rain, clad

in oilskins and lulled by the rhythmic slapping of the
wipers, with the vague intention of exploring the old
mine he'd passed on the way to Roger Trevenney's. Butts
had confirmed that this was the presumed location of
Ruth Trevenney's murder. But on the spur of the moment,
he changed his mind and decided to pay a visit to the
Porters.

The little group of cottages at the base of Towey Head
looked drab and forlorn in the teeming rain. The Porters'
back garden resembled a mud wallow for hippopotami
with bits of green poking out here and there. Powell
knocked on the door. He glanced next door. There was no
sign of Dr. Harris's car, and he wondered if he was off
ministering to Roger Trevenney. Linda Porter's face
appeared in the window. There was a flicker of recognition, then the door opened. She was dressed in jeans and
a bulky sweater, her hair pulled primly back.

"Chief Superintendent, this is a surprise. You'd better
come in or you'll catch your death. Here, let me take
your jacket. To what do I owe this, um, pleasure?"

"I just happened to be in the neighborhood," Powell
said lamely.

She smiled. "Well, I must have made quite an impression on you."

"It's my bulbs, actually."

"I beg your pardon?"

"With all this rain I'm worried the rot's set in. Back in
the garden in London, I mean. I wanted some advice."

She laughed doubtfully. "Your must be joking! What's
this all about?"

Powell serious now. "It's a technique they teach us at

police school to put someone at ease when you're about to interview them."

She looked at him. "Oh, I see. You'd better come and sit down, then."

The tiny living room looked even more shabby than Powell remembered it. "By the way, is Mr. Porter about?" he said.

"Gone to the village."

"I'll get right to the point, Mrs. Porter—"

"Would you care for a drink, Chief Superintendent?"

"Er, no, thank you."

"I'll have one, if you don't mind."

She got up, poured herself half a glass of gin, and returned to her chair. She pulled her long legs under her. "You were saying, Chief Superintendent . . . ?"

He studied her closely. "I imagine you've heard about Nick Tebble."

She brushed an invisible strand of hair from her face. "Yes, it's terrible isn't it? A quiet little village like Penrick—to think that there's somebody around here who could do something like that."

"Had you ever met him?"

"I'd pass him on the road occasionally or see him in the village, that's about it. I got the impression he tended to keep his own company."

"That's what everyone keeps telling me. Did he ever come here, Mrs. Porter?"

She thought for a moment. "Not that I know of, but you could check with Jim." She met his eyes with a steady gaze.

"I'll do that." Powell was beginning to have second thoughts. She was either a consummate actor, or perhaps

Black had been mistaken about Tebble's skiff. Or if it was Tebble's boat, he supposed there could be another explanation for its presence near the Porters' cottage that morning. He wasn't convinced one way or the other at this point.

"I get the distinct impression you're driving at something, Chief Superintendent. Why don't you just ask me straight out?"

"Perhaps that would be best, Mrs. Porter." He cursed silently. He had hoped to catch her unprepared, but she had either anticipated his strategy or was simply being forthright. "My associate, Sergeant Black, had occasion to be in this neck of the woods on Saturday morning around ten o'clock. He had intended to pop in and ask you a few questions, but he indicated that you, er, had a visitor at the time."

If Powell had been looking for a reaction, he could not have been disappointed.

She turned as white as a ghost. "It's—it's not—not what you think . . . I mean Jim and I, we . . . he must have been mistaken . . ." She drew her arms around herself.

"Nick Tebble's boat was pulled up on the beach not fifty yards from here," Powell persisted.

She looked at him incredulously. "Nick Tebble?" Then suddenly a flash of comprehension in her face. "You don't mean . . . I can't believe you thought that I . . ." She looked at Powell, shaking her head slowly. "I don't know whether to laugh or cry. My God, Chief Superintendent, it wasn't Nick Tebble!"

"Who, then?"

"I don't see that my personal affairs are any of your business." A hint of defiance echoed in her voice.

An interesting choice of words, he thought. "My business, Mrs. Porter, is finding out who murdered Tebble."

She averted her eyes. "Would you promise not to tell anyone?"

Powell's tone turned sharp now. "This is a murder investigation, not a bloody pajama party."

"Jim would kill me if he found out."

"Perhaps you should have thought about that before you—"

"The last thing I need is a sermon from you! I suppose you're as pure as the driven snow!" Her eyes flashed angrily.

Powell did not think a reply necessary. For the first time he became aware of a clock ticking somewhere in the house. He counted the seconds to himself, as if reciting a mantra.

Eventually, Linda Porter broke the silence. "I can't tell you. Surely you can understand that."

Powell sighed wearily. "Let me review the facts, Mrs. Porter. Nick Tebble's boat was seen parked outside your cottage Saturday morning while you were engaged in sexual relations with somebody inside. And I'm assuming from what you've already told me that it wasn't your husband. If you were with Tebble, you may have been one of the last persons to see him alive."

"Sexual *relations*? What a quaint phrase. All right, Chief Superintendent, I'll satisfy your voyeuristic appetite. I don't know whose bloody boat it was, but I bloody well know who was screwing me! It was Tony Rowlands, if you must know."

* * *

As Powell drove back to Penrick the visibility was reduced to no more than a few feet, and the rain was drumming a loud tattoo on the roof of the car. Even with the wipers at full speed, he could hardly see where he was going. Linda Porter's revelation had thrown him off balance. He realized that he would have to talk to Rowlands again at some point, although there was probably no rush now; she would no doubt get to him first. Handling Jim Porter, the cuckolded husband, would be trickier. The direct approach would no doubt be decidedly unpleasant for both of them. For obvious reasons, he normally preferred to hold off in such cases until he'd determined whether any information the husband could provide was relevant to the investigation. In this instance, however, Porter may have witnessed his wife's indiscretion, which opened up some interesting possibilities—

Powell's train of thought was interrupted as the car plunged abruptly into a vast puddle of indeterminate depth. A sheet of muddy water smacked the windscreen, completely obscuring his view of the road ahead. He dared not stop with the wheels churning and slipping in the soft mud. Eventually he felt the tires begin to grip on harder ground, and the car lurched slowly ahead up an incline. Suddenly, there was a glare of lights through the blurred windscreen and a horn tooting insistently.

Instinctively Powell wrenched the steering wheel over, sending the car into the ditch with a jarring thump. A battered Land Rover rattled by, passing mere inches from Powell's right wing mirror. He caught an impression of a man driving, staring fixedly ahead. Powell's heart pounded as he attempted to regain his composure. He could have sworn the driver was Jim Porter.

*   *   *

Having prevailed upon a local farmer to pull him out of the ditch with his tractor, Powell eventually arrived back at the Wrecker's Rest, soaked to the skin and in a foul mood. Mr. and Mrs. Polfrock parted like the Red Sea as he stormed up to his room. After a hot bath and not a little reflection on the morning's events, Powell, blissfully heedless of Robbie Burns's advice to mice and men, had decided on a plan of action. It was almost noon, so he wandered downstairs on the off chance that either Black or Butts had returned for lunch. They had agreed, after the appropriate assurances from Butts that there would be no more unpleasant surprises of any kind, that in light of recent developments it would be prudent to transfer their base of operations from the pub to the guesthouse.

Sergeant Black and Chief Inspector Butts were already in attendance when Powell strolled into the dining room. Engaged in an animated conversation, they looked up only when Powell sat down.

"I hope I'm not interrupting anything," he said dryly. "What's on the menu?"

Black grinned. "Chicken *Madras*, sir."

Powell glared at him. "Don't toy with my emotions, Black. I'm in no mood."

"Black mentioned that you liked curry, sir," Butts piped in, looking pleased with himself, "so I, er, took the liberty of mentioning it to Agnes and she's whipped something up."

Good Christ, Powell thought, they'll kill me with kindness. "Splendid," he said unconvincingly.

"While we're waiting, I've got a few things to report," Butts continued. "You remember Katherine Reynolds, our missing boater from Torquay? Her fiancé has identified the ring on the hand we found in Tebble's cellar as belonging to her. And I just got word from Forensics on the cart; they managed to come up with some fiber samples that are similar to the kapok in the life jacket she was wearing."

Black grunted with satisfaction. "So our theory about Tebble and the Riddle was right."

"It looks that way," Butts said. "There's one more thing." He concluded with admirable efficiency, "the police surgeon has filed his report on Tebble. He puts the time of death somewhere between noon and two o'clock Saturday afternoon."

"Anything else turn up at the Old Fish Cellar?" Powell asked.

Butts shook his head. "We're still working on it."

"How about you, Black? Find any smut?"

Black chortled. "Not exactly, sir. But I did have a chat with Mrs. Halford, the proprietor of the teahouse. Nice old lady, likes to talk. Anyway, she let slip that somebody offered to sell her a barrel of sherry a couple of years ago. You wouldn't like to guess who it was, would you, sir?"

"You know I don't like guessing games, Black."

"Our friend next door, Tony Rowlands."

"Why am I not surprised?" He looked at Butts. "Do you know anything about this?"

Butts looked a little sheepish. "Well, sir, it's no secret that sort of thing goes on."

"You're not going to start making excuses, are you, Butts?"

"I suppose I was, in a way, sir. These days we barely have enough manpower to deal with the big things and we're not able to do a very good job of it."

"What else is new?" Powell sighed.

"There's something else, Mr. Powell," Black went on. "I bumped into Jenny Thompson at the teahouse. I took her aside and had a word with her. She claims that Rowlands was at the pub all day Saturday. When he wasn't working out front, he was in the back doing the books."

"That's interesting. Tell me, Butts, do you know anything about her living arrangements?"

"I understand she has a room above the pub."

"What about Rowlands?"

"The same, as far as I know."

"I wonder if they share the same bathroom."

Butts shrugged. "It wouldn't surprise me."

"We'd better follow that up," Powell said. He then went on to describe his interview with Linda Porter that morning and his subsequent close encounter with her husband on the drive back to the village.

Black extended his lower lip thoughtfully. "I wonder if her husband saw the boat?"

Powell's response was cut short by the arrival of Mrs. Polfrock with the promised chicken *Madras*. They made polite noises as they tucked in, tentatively at first, then with increasing enthusiasm. Powell had to admit that it wasn't half bad. The curry sauce had no doubt come from a tin, but, after all, it's the thought that counts. The only thing missing was Mr. Polfrock playing the sitar in the corner.

There was a sudden flurry of activity in the front hall, and a moment later Mrs. Polfrock was hurrying back to their table. "A telephone message for you, Chief Superintendent," she said breathlessly. "From Roger Trevenney. He said to come quickly—he said it was urgent!"

CHAPTER 16

Powell wasn't looking forward to the drive out to Roger Trevenney's cottage, but the rain had let up to an intermittent drizzle and there was a hint of brightness in the western sky. He switched on his mental automatic pilot, and before he knew it he was turning into Trevenney's driveway.

He knocked on the door but there was no response. He waited a few seconds and then knocked again, louder and more persistently this time. He wondered if Trevenney had gone out, but soon he heard a faint noise behind the door. A few moments later the door opened slowly, and Trevenney, gray faced and gaunt, was bracing himself against the door frame, motioning for Powell to come in.

"Here, let me help you, sir," Powell said, concern in his voice.

Trevenney waved him off and shuffled slowly down the hall, holding one hand against the wall, with Powell close behind him. At the sitting room door, he turned, staggered a few feet into the room, and then collapsed into an armchair.

Powell could hardly believe it was the same man he had spoken to yesterday. He stood over Trevenney, who was breathing heavily, eyes closed. "Can I get you something? A glass of water or a cup of tea?"

Trevenney slowly opened his eyes. "You're most kind, but no, thank you," he said, his voice barely more than a whisper. "Thank you for coming so quickly. I'm not sure how long I can . . . I mean to say there is something I must tell you."

"Perhaps I should call Dr. Harris . . ." Powell volunteered.

Trevenney smiled weakly. "Peter was out to see me this morning. That man should have been somebody's mother. Don't worry yourself, Chief Superintendent. As I explained yesterday, I have good days and bad days. This is one of my bad days. I'll be all right."

Powell was doubtful but realized there was little he could do. Trevenney had closed his eyes again. Powell quietly pulled up a chair and sat down opposite the old man. "You said it was urgent, sir," he prompted gently.

Trevenney opened his eyes again and looked at Powell. "I was going to tell you yesterday, but I—I lost my . . . I mean to say it somehow slipped my mind. I can't imagine how."

"You can tell me now, Mr. Trevenney."

"Yes, I must. But please call me Roger. I think we know each other well enough by now, don't you?"

Powell smiled. "Of course we do, Roger. My name is Erskine by the way."

This seemed to make the old man happy. He pushed himself up in his chair with renewed vigor. "It was when we were talking about the second possibility."

"I'm trying to recall . . ."

Trevenney drew a shallow breath. "The possibility that Nick Tebble knew the identity of Ruth's murderer."

"Oh, yes. Go on."

"It's the telephone call, you see."

"Telephone call?"

"I received a call. From a man. He said he had Ruth's diary. He said it provided the key to the identity of her killer. He said he would call me again, then he rang off."

"When did this happen?"

"That's the part I'm not sure about. It's my damned head, not working properly, you see. I think it was about a week ago, but sometimes it feels like it was yesterday, or a year ago. I don't know. Time seems all jumbled up these days." He shook his head in exasperation.

Powell leaned forward. "I want you to think about this very carefully. Did you receive this phone call before or after you first heard about the Riddle?"

Trevenney's face contorted as he tried to concentrate. "I remember I was very distraught at the time. Before receiving the call, I mean. So I'm sure it was afterward."

"You said it was a man. Are you certain?"

"I think so. But the voice was sort of muffled."

"Any distinguishing characteristics, an accent, anything like that?"

Trevenney looked crestfallen. "I'm sorry, I just can't remember."

Powell experienced a sinking feeling. "Did this person ever call back?"

"No. Do you think he will?" His eyes hopeful.

"I wouldn't be a bit surprised," Powell lied.

Trevenney seemed to brighten slightly at the prospect.

"When he does, I'll make detailed notes so you'll have something more to go on."

"That's the ticket."

"Before you go, Erskine, I feel bound to tell you that I haven't been entirely forthright with you."

"Oh?"

"I mean, I'm not the long-suffering saint I might appear to be at first glance."

"Roger, you needn't—"

"No, I'm simply a father like any other. You must have children of your own . . ."

Powell swallowed. "Yes, two boys."

"Fine lads, no doubt?"

Powell nodded.

"Then you can imagine what it's been like for me all these years. Do you know what kept me going?" A feverish intensity in his voice.

Powell stared at him.

"Revenge. The thought that I might one day get my hands on the bastard that killed my Ruth. Does that surprise you?"

"It would surprise me if you didn't feel that way."

Trevenney sagged into his chair. He closed his eyes again and sighed deeply. "Thank you for letting me get that off my chest. I know I can rest easy now."

"I'll do my best, Roger. I promise."

"I know you will." A long pause. "Goodbye, Erskine."

Powell was deeply troubled; he had a feeling he would not see Roger Trevenney again.

On the way back to the village, Powell turned in to see Dr. Harris. "I missed you this morning," he said simply.

Harris looking at him strangely. "I went to see Roger."

"Yes, I know. I've just come from there. He's very bad, isn't he?"

Harris nodded. "I've just made arrangements to have him moved to hospital in St. Ives. He'll be better off there."

"I don't think he's going to like the idea much."

"I'm only doing what I think is best for him," Harris said stiffly.

"Yes, yes of course you are."

A strained silence.

Eventually Powell spoke, "This may not seem like the appropriate time, but I must ask you something."

"Yes."

"You mentioned before that you'd never seen Nick Tebble over at the Porters'. What about Tony Rowlands?"

"Do you mind me asking what this is all about?"

"I shouldn't have thought you'd need to ask."

"I've never been much of a busybody, Chief Inspector."

"For Christ's sake, just answer the question!" Powell exploded.

Harris was clearly taken aback. "No, I haven't seen Rowlands next door, actually."

"Has Mrs. Porter had *any* gentleman callers in the last month or so?"

Harris thought about it for a moment. "There was someone about a week ago—I remember now—it was young Wilcox."

"Was Mr. Porter home at the time?"

"I can't remember. I'm sorry."

"There's just one more thing. You said you went to see Roger Saturday morning. Do you remember what time you drove back?"

"Sometime between noon and one o'clock, I think."

"You didn't happen to pass anyone, did you?"

He frowned. "Why, yes, I did meet someone on the road."

Powell waited.

"It was George Polfrock."

"Going the other way?"

"Yes."

Powell sighed. "Thank you, Dr. Harris."

"This is about Ruth, isn't it?"

"It's always been about Ruth."

"I'm sorry about before . . ." His eyes watery.

Powell placed his hand on the doctor's shoulder. "I'm the one who should apologize. Now, go and see to your friend."

When Powell got back to the guesthouse, he cornered George Polfrock in the front hall. The elusive proprietor of the Wrecker's Rest, upon spotting Powell coming through the front door, had been about to duck into the dining room, but Mrs. Polfrock, who happened to be coming out at the same time, provided a fortuitous and formidable barrier.

"I was just going to have a word with your husband, Mrs. Polfrock," Powell remarked breezily.

Mrs. Polfrock's eyes narrowed. "Would you like me to sit it? Perhaps I could . . ."

Powell winked at her. "Man talk, I'm afraid."

She turned on Mr. Polfrock and glared at him. "When you're done, I've got some chores for you to do."

Powell noticed that Mr. Polfrock wasn't exactly turning cartwheels across the floor at the prospect of being interviewed, and he had definitely turned a whiter shade of pale. "Now, then, why don't we step into the Residents' Lounge, Mr. Polfrock?"

The little man acquiesced silently, resigned apparently to whatever the fates had in store for him.

Powell arranged two chairs so that the escritoire in the corner of the room would be within view of them both and then invited Mr. Polfrock to sit down. He took a seat opposite and smiled evenly. "I've been looking forward to having this little chat for quite some time now."

"Oh?" Mr. Polfrock said in a small voice.

"You don't mind if I smoke?"

Mr. Polfrock looked alarmed. "Agnes doesn't . . ."

Powell lit a cigarette and reached over to the coffee table for a saucer to use as an ashtray. "Now, George, where to begin? You don't mind if I call you George?"

Mr. Polfrock shook his head nervously.

"You aren't a shooting man, by any chance, are you, George?"

Polfrock swallowed hard, seemingly unable to speak.

"Great sport, shooting. I have an old Westley Richards detachable lock gun. Inherited it from my father. It's over sixty years old, but it's as sound as the day it was built. Do you know what a gun like that costs nowadays? Five thousand pounds, I reckon, twenty thousand for a new one. I certainly couldn't afford it. Makes one think, doesn't it, George? One should really keep a gun like that locked up, don't you think? Any gun, for that matter. One can't be too careful with all the break-ins and burglaries these days. You don't happen to own a shotgun, do you, George?"

Polfrock, slack-jawed, stared at Powell as if mesmerized.

Powell drew thoughtfully on his cigarette. "There's something decidedly Freudian about a gun," he went on.

"In any case, one should really have a gun safe. Like that one over there." He motioned casually toward the escritoire.

Polfrock began to gulp spasmodically like a fish out of water. "It—it was y-you!" he stammered. "I forget to lock the safe, just the once, and . . . Do you realize that I haven't been able to sleep wondering who . . ."

"My wife is always getting after me for rearranging things around the house. I seem to have this compulsion to turn things topsy-turvy. But look at the bright side, George—better me than Mrs. Polfrock. A stroke of luck, you might say."

Polfrock colored. "My God! If Agnes ever found out, she'd kill me!"

Powell smiled. "Surely not, Mr. Polfrock. Your wife strikes me as a reasonable woman."

Polfrock looked terrified. "What do you want from me? I've burned the whole lot. I've learned my lesson, I promise you!"

Powell didn't believe a word of it. He fixed him with a distasteful look.

Polfrock imploring now. "Look, I'd do anything to keep her from finding out!"

"Anything, George?"

"What do you mean by that?"

"Where were you on Saturday afternoon between noon and four o'clock?"

"I can't remember, I—"

"I'd advise you to try," Powell said sharply.

"Oh, I remember now! I was up along Mawgawan Beach. Bird-watching." He made an almost comical attempt to sound blasé.

A knowing smile from Powell. "Exactly what kind of birds were you watching, George?"

"I don't know what you mean!"

"Tony Rowlands tells me there's a group of kids camping out there."

"Oh, him."

"You didn't happen to see Nick Tebble on Saturday, by any chance?"

"No, of course not, that's the day he was . . ." A look of panic.

"Yes?"

"I hardly knew him!"

Powell sighed. "How long have you lived here, George?"

"All my life," he said grudgingly.

"I don't suppose you knew Ruth Trevenney, either."

A long pause then an inaudible response.

"You'll have to speak up, George."

"Yes, I knew her."

Powell leaned back in his chair, assessing Polfrock's demeanor. Mined out, Powell concluded, like all the tin mines in Cornwall. "There's just one more thing, George."

There was an anxious look in Polfrock's eyes.

"The magazines. Rowlands gets them for you, doesn't he?"

Polfrock hesitated, then he nodded weakly.

Powell gestured in a dismissive manner. "Watch yourself, George."

After Polfrock fled the room, Powell sat motionless in his chair. Eventually, he lit another cigarette. There was a movement at the door. He looked up. It was Butts.

"We've found something, sir. At the Old Fish Cellar. Nearly ten thousand quid hidden under the floor."

CHAPTER 17

"If it wasn't for the bloody Riddle, this would be a relatively straightforward case," Butts asserted. "At least the line of inquiry would be obvious. Linda Porter is fooling around with Rowlands. Her husband comes home unannounced on Saturday morning and catches them in the act, but mistakenly thinks it's Tebble. Before he can confront them, he's interrupted by Black, here. Porter stews about it for a while then drives out to the Old Fish Cellar later that afternoon and does our Nick." Butts paused to take a swig of ale from a long-necked brown bottle. He had persuaded his sister-in-law to provide some suitable refreshment to lubricate the mental processes. "Or maybe," he continued, "it was Tebble who was shagging her, and Rowlands is the jealous one."

Black looked doubtful. "There has to be more to it than that. The Riddle, all that money, it can't be a coincidence. What about the phone call to Roger Trevenney about Ruth's diary? Perhaps it was Tebble. If he knew something about Ruth's murder, he could have been blackmailing someone. That would explain the money."

Butts shook his head. "That money's been there for quite some time, by the looks of it. One of my lads is a numismatist; just by looking at 'em he reckons the notes are more than twenty years old. We're checking the serial numbers. If Tebble was a collector, himself, he had a penchant for ten-pound notes. And there's one more thing, sir. I did a bit more poking around out there, as you suggested. Behind the shed under a tarp there's a pile of old logs with some black stuff that looks like shoelaces growing all over it."

"Rhizomorphs," Powell observed sagely. He leaned back in his chair. "So what have we got? Tebble concocts the Riddle to draw attention to Ruth Trevenney's murder. Roger Trevenney gets a call recently from someone who claims to have information that implicates his daughter's killer. Jim Porter discovers, if he didn't already know, that his wife has been unfaithful with Tebble, or Rowlands, or God knows who else. Tebble is killed and we discover that he's been sitting on a tidy sum of money at the Old Fish Cellar. Rowlands, at least, appears to have an alibi of sorts. Have I missed anything?"

"I still think we need to follow up on the smuggling angle, sir," Black said.

Powell nodded. "Butts, I think it might be best if you talked to Rowlands about that. You know the territory better than we do. And determine his whereabouts Saturday afternoon. He could easily have slipped out for the half hour it would have taken to drive out to Tebble's, do the job, and get back to the Head."

"Right."

Black looked disappointed.

"Cheer up, Bill. I've got a juicy one for you. I'd like you to talk to Jim Porter. We need to confirm whether it was him you saw ducking up the back lane on Saturday. It's clearly a crucial point. See how he reacts, then proceed as you see fit."

Black, apparently mollified, nodded.

"Also, have a word with Colin Wilcox. According to Dr. Harris, Wilcox has been out to the Porters' recently. Find out why."

Black grinned. "No need, sir. I ran into him in the High Street yesterday. Young Wilcox seems to know his way around Penrick, so in a roundabout way I took the liberty of questioning him about the Porters. He wasn't able to add much, but during the course of the conversation it came out that he'd been out to the Porters' recently to quote on a plumbing job."

"That's interesting. The Porters don't have indoor plumbing, as far as I know."

Black shrugged. "Maybe they're thinking of having it put in."

"Perhaps. Did you believe him?"

"I didn't have any reason not to, sir."

"It seems to me it's a question of motive," Butts ventured. "If, for the sake of argument, Tebble was using the Riddle to blackmail someone in connection with Ruth Trevenney's murder, why kill him after the fact?"

"Perhaps he raised the stakes."

"What do you mean, sir?"

Powell frowned. "To be quite honest, I'm not sure what I mean. I think we'd better just take it a step at a time and see what develops."

*"Come what come may, time and the hour runs
through the roughest day,"* Black intoned solemnly.

"Powell—this is a pleasant surprise." Jane Goode
opened the door wide. "Welcome to my garret."

An unmade bed, lunch dishes, books and papers strewn
everywhere.

"How goes the novel?"

She sighed. "It's coming, but so's my deadline. How
are things with you?"

"Getting interesting. I was hoping I could persuade
you to take tomorrow off."

She looked at him doubtfully. "What did you have in
mind?"

"I've been meaning to have a look around the old mine
where Ruth Trevenney . . . I mean, it wouldn't be quite as
grim as it sounds," he went on quickly. "I thought it
would be a break for you. We could pack a lunch, do a bit
of exploring."

She thought about it for a moment. "I'd love to, I
really would, but I *am* under the gun, I've only got three
weeks."A strained silence.

"Of course, I understand perfectly. Well, I'll leave you
to it, then." He felt like an idiot.

Jane Goode closed the door slowly and reluctantly.

The next morning around ten o'clock, Powell set out
on the loop road. The sky was gray and equivocal. There
was nothing on the radio and his mind was in a turmoil.
What was it that Black had said? Something had twigged
at the time, but he couldn't quite put his finger on it. All
he knew was, something didn't fit. It was as if he was

dealing with two entirely separate cases, two lines that converged at the death of Nick Tebble; a contemporary tale of adultery and jealousy, and a murder that happened thirty years ago. Was Tebble killed because somebody thought he'd been screwing around with Linda Porter, or was it because he'd known something about Ruth's murder? Or were the two questions somehow related? Powell braked suddenly.

Just past the turning to Dr. Harris's, a well-used Land Rover was parked beside the road and a man was digging out the mouth of a drainage ditch at the point where it discharged from the adjacent field into the roadside ditch. It was Jim Porter.

Against his better judgment Powell slowed to a stop, on the pretext of asking directions to the mine. He got out of the car. "Good morning," he said.

Porter leaned awkwardly on his shovel and nodded warily. In response to Powell's query, he uttered some terse directions.

"I spoke to your wife yesterday . . ." Powell remarked. He left it open-ended.

"She didn't mention it."

"We'd like to have a word with you about Nick Tebble."

"I'm rather busy right now . . ."

Powell smiled. "I understand. My associate, Detective-Sergeant Black, was hoping to catch up with you later today, if it's convenient."

Porter shrugged. "I'm not going anywhere." He shifted his weight from one foot to the other.

"He went to see you at your cottage Saturday morning, but there didn't seem to be anyone around."

Porter's eyes narrowed. "He should bloody well call first, then, shouldn't he?"

"It was about this time of the morning, as I recall," Powell continued.

"What are you playing at?" Porter snapped.

"I beg your pardon?"

"Do you think it's easy? Trying to make your own way in life when they want you to fail. When everyone's against you, bloody everyone! I've heard the gossip—I know what people are saying. But I'm not stupid. Do you think I don't know what's going on? You don't have to rub my nose in it!" His eyes turned wild. "I'm not going to stand for any more of it, I tell you!" Tears welled up. He suddenly lifted his shovel, brandishing it at port arms.

Here, thought Powell, is a man at the end of his rope. He made some soothing noises and departed as decorously as possible under the circumstances. A quick call on his mobile phone to alert Black to Porter's emotional state. Best to hold off for the time being, he decided. He put it as tactfully as possible. He was stealing Black's thunder in a sense, but it was evident that Porter would need careful handling. The man was clearly over the edge, and Powell had little doubt that in his present state of mind he was quite capable of committing an irrational act. But murder? he wondered.

He passed the turning to the Old Fish Cellar and then swung east on a rough, overgrown track that headed off into the hills. Just ahead, beyond a slight rise, he could see the upper brick portion of the round chimney that marked the location of the old engine house. He drew up to a rusted wire mesh fence marked with a faded sign that announced somewhat ambiguously: DANGER KEEP OUT.

The fence had fallen down in several places and he had no difficulty finding a place to get through. The view to the southwest was spectacular, a steep grassy slope speckled with wildflowers, then the edge of the cliffs and the sea below. The road back toward Penrick was hidden behind a small hill. He tried to visualize the miles of shafts and tunnels lying beneath his feet and to imagine the life of a Cornish tin miner a hundred years ago. Adits sunk beneath the ore bodies and draining to the sea were used to de-water the shafts where the miners worked. Shafts sunk below the drainage level were pumped by steam engines in the engine houses. In some cases, the workings extended for several fathoms below the seabed itself, and he had read somewhere that the miners could hear the sound of the surf crashing above them.

Powell walked over to the engine house. It was remarkably well preserved and largely intact. Roofless, the building itself and the lower two-thirds of the cylindrical chimney were built of gray granite stone, the upper part of red brick. He peered into the gloom. The opening of the shaft work appeared to be boarded over, for safety reasons he presumed.

He spent the next half hour looking around the mine site. He could hear the occasional car passing by on the road. There was a variety of rusting machine parts strewn about the site whose precise origin and function were the subjects of considerable speculation on his part. And there were numerous shallow depressions in the ground, spaced randomly as far as he could tell, each about ten feet in diameter and choked with gorse and brambles. Some were marked with faded DANGER signs, some not. These marked the location, he guessed, of old shafts. He though about Ruth Trevenney. He wondered which one of the depressions concealed the tunnel that opened to the sea in the cliffs near Mawgawan Beach. He realized now that he should have asked Butts for more specific directions, although locating the exact spot where Ruth's body had been hidden seemed a bit academic three decades after the fact. He thought about it for a moment. Many of the shafts, if not all of them, were presumably drained by the same adit system. Drop something down any one of them and it might well end up in the sea eventually.

He sat down on a rock and lit a cigarette. He looked at the sky. Dark and ominous. If he didn't shift he was going to get wet. A raw, gusty wind had picked up, and he felt the first drops of rain. He got to his feet and turned up his collar. Just as he was about to start back for his car, he noticed a larger patch of brush just beyond the engine house. He decided to investigate.

It was really more of an overgrown swale about thirty feet in diameter with gently sloping sides covered in brambles and gorse bushes that were nearly as tall as a man on the bottom. The ground was slightly mounded around the perimeter of the depression, with the exception of the uphill side, where periodic runoff from the hillside above had eroded a channel. Could it be? Powell wondered. One could easily imagine the opening of a shaft beneath the tangle of brush. Starting in from the edge, Powell picked his way carefully through the brambles. The depression had a gravelly bed sloping slightly inward toward the center. The wind was moaning steadily now, driving the rain in dark sheets across the hillside.

Stumbling slightly, he felt something catch his leg, then the tearing of cloth and skin against a thorny branch.

He looked at his trousers and swore; he'd only just bought the bloody things a month ago. He bent down to inspect the damage. Had he not been so fastidious, he might have noticed the slight movement behind him. As it was, the blow caught him on the back of the head just as he started to look around. He fell forward, arms flailing amongst the branches.

As unconsciousness filled his head like an expanding cloud of black ink, he experienced the curious sensation of not stopping where the ground should have been.

CHAPTER 18

The next thing Powell was aware of was an excruci-
ating pain in his right knee and a pounding in his head.
He lay on his right side on a bed that was hard as rock.
He could hear the hollow sound of water trickling in the
darkness and there was a salty taste in his mouth. He held
his hand up in front of his face. Nothing. He suppressed a
rush of panic. Perhaps he was only dreaming. He turned
his head painfully. There was a suggestion of something
above him. He blinked slowly. A diffuse smudge of
brightness on the ceiling like a moonlit skylight and faint
streaks of reflected light down dark, shiny walls. Where
am I? he wondered groggily. He closed his eyes and tried
to think. His head whirled and he could hear the blood
roaring in his ears amidst a hundred jumbled associa-
tions. He opened his eyes again and attempted to get his
bearings. He stared at the fuzzy light above him, imagining that it was bathing his pineal gland with revitalizing
rays—or was it the pituitary gland? He slowly began to
remember. Driving to the mine that morning, smoking a
cigarette in the rain, thrashing through the thorn bushes,

and then falling . . . He supposed he must have tripped on something. Suddenly, the sobering certainty of it, dashing any remaining hopes that he might simply be having a nightmare. Good Christ, he realized, I've fallen down a bloody mine shaft!

Breathing deeply, he took a moment to take stock. He decided that he'd better not try anything rash, like moving more than an inch. He felt light-headed, and the whimsical thought occurred to him that he could already be in purgatory, in which case he might just as well pop over the edge to check out the next level of the Inferno. Best not to jump to conclusions, though. Besides, it was too bloody cold—no fire and brimstone within a hundred miles. He slowly straightened his legs. A stab of pain in his right knee induced an involuntary grunt, the sound reverberating eerily in the gloom. He'd twisted something, all right. He groped with his left arm behind his back. There was a smooth rock wall, cold and damp. Then he felt around in front of him. There was an impression of another wall, too far away to reach. His vision was slightly blurred. He blinked several times, but it didn't help. He touched the rock on which he lay. It had a gritty texture. He slid his hand slowly away from him, stretching his arm out. The rock ended abruptly about two and a half feet away; there was just a rough edge and then nothing. He shifted position slightly so that he could reach down with his forearm over the edge. A vertical wall like the one behind him. Not daring to think about what it meant, he felt around for a pebble but could find nothing large enough. He reached into his trouser pocket and extracted a coin. He held his breath and dropped it over the edge. Silence for a few seconds and then a faint tinkle far below.

It was pretty clear he was in the soup. For all practical purposes, a bottomless pit below, a sheer rock wall above, and him marooned on a narrow ledge, perhaps four feet wide if he was lucky. His own little world perched between Heaven and Hell. The question was, How precisely had he got there? He surmised that he must have broken through the overgrown opening of the shaft and fallen some distance before ending up in his present location. So far so good. But he couldn't have fallen very far or he wouldn't have been in any condition to be contemplating the problem. Using his right arm, he levered himself painfully over onto his back. He tried to relax his cramping muscles.

His eyes were growing accustomed to the attenuated light, and he was able to get some impression of the rock wall above him. Illuminated faintly from above, the face gleamed dully. He could see occasional darker striations that looked like cracks or shallow fissures. The light source was obviously the sky behind the screen of branches that covered the mouth of the shaft. It was difficult to say whether the opening was fifteen or fifty feet above him. Closer to the former, he reckoned, considering the fact that he had survived the fall more or less intact. He suddenly realized what a close call it had been. To have hit the ledge in the first place, and then to have remained there, was something of a minor miracle.

He thought about what to do next. He didn't see that he had much choice in the matter other than to sit tight. Thank God he had told Jane he was going to the mine; they would undoubtedly come looking for him. He held his wrist close to his eyes. He searched the inscrutable face of his watch and then felt the broken crystal with his fingers. He guessed it was sometime in the midafternoon. He thought about Marion and the boys—quickly calculating the time difference—who were no doubt still happily tucked into their beds at the Château Whistler. Just as well they were away and wouldn't have to worry. Might as well get comfortable, he thought. He pushed himself into a sitting position with his back against the rock and his legs slightly bent. He winced as he touched his swollen knee.

He closed his eyes and waited, his head aching fiercely, lulled by the pervasive murmur of running water. He didn't think anything of it until he felt the first cold trickle running down his neck. He shifted position only to find himself sitting in a puddle. He swore and struggled painfully to his feet. He looked up. The rock looked different now, shimmering in the gloom with a shiny glaze. He reached up and touched the wall. He could feel water running over his fingers and down his sleeve. He could hear it splashing on the ledge. He tried to think. It had been raining, he remembered; he could visualize the low berm of earth around the depression in the ground and the signs of erosion on the slope above. The berm had obviously been intended to divert runoff around the opening of the shaft, but since the upper side had been breached, any runoff from the hillside above would tend to collect in the depression and then flow down the shaft.

He began to consider the potential implications of this and was at the point of wondering just how bad it could get when the trickle suddenly became a torrent. A sheet of water splashed down the wall, and although he moved as close to the edge of the ledge as he dared, he was soon drenched to the bone. He began to shiver convulsively. He would bloody well die of exposure at this rate. For the first time he noticed that the ledge was curved, about ten feet long and petering out at both ends. He knew that in the old days the miners had used long ladders to descend into and ascend from the mines each day. Strangely detached, he wondered if the ledge had something to do with ladders. He stared down into the blackness. It was the snakes that had him worried. His head was spinning. He knew now that he had to get out, that he couldn't afford to wait any longer. But he couldn't remember why. The idea had entered his mind fully formed, as it were, and when he tried to analyze it, the reasons eluded him. He just knew that he had to move.

Facing the wall, and steadying himself with his right hand, he shuffled stiffly to his left, stopping a pace away from where the ledge, now only about two feet wide, ended abruptly. He pressed closely against the rock. He was no longer being showered with cold spray, and the curve of wall to his left looked dry. It appeared that the water was only flowing down the side of the shaft on which the ledge was situated—the uphill side in relation to the topography aboveground, presumably. Just beyond the end of the ledge there was a thin shadow—it looked like a crack or fault in the shaft wall—that ascended vertically for several feet before veering off to the right. The upper few feet of the crack were indistinct in the wash of light immediately below the opening of the shaft, but it appeared to continue right to the top.

One more careful step to the left and he could reach out with his left hand to feel the crack. His fingers curled around the edge. Three to four inches wide and just about as deep. He reached up as far as he could. It seemed fairly uniform. He ran his hand over the wall between him and the crack. Rough with the occasional small nubbin to serve as a hold. He felt slightly giddy but, once again, without being able to think about it rationally, he knew what he had to do. Right foot on the end of the ledge, left hand grasping the edge of the crack at about head height, straddle the intervening section of wall with his left leg and then jam his foot in the crack. Pull himself over, get his right hand in quickly above his left and his right foot above the left one. Should be a piece of cake, he thought illogically.

The problem was somewhat reminiscent of the Moonlight Sonata on Scafell, a climb he had pioneered with his mates in the Cambridge Mountaineering Club. Not as difficult as it looked—a "Hard Very Severe" at most—but very exposed, and accomplished at night after having consumed considerably more beer than was prudent under the circumstances. It did not, however, seem to occur to him that his knee was an unknown quantity, that brogues were not the most suitable footwear for rock climbing, and that he would have no rope to stop him should he fall.

He again reached out with his left hand and grasped the edge of the crack. He swung his left leg out with a painful grunt, taking all of his weight on his right leg. Could be worse, he thought grimly. Gritting his teeth, he somehow managed to wedge his shoe into the crack. His heart was racing and he was breathing rapidly. He was committed now, spread-eagled on the face between the crack and the ledge, the abyss below. The next move would be the tricky one. It is a maxim in rock climbing that one endeavors at all times to maintain three points of contact with the rock; that is, one only moves one hand or foot at a time. Then if one of the three holds fails, the climber still has two points of contact to prevent a fall. In this instance, he had to move his right hand and right foot over to the crack more or less simultaneously, pulling himself over with his left hand and taking most of his weight on his left foot.

He made an effort to concentrate on his breathing, trying not to think about the drop below him. He exhaled sharply, then with a decisive movement swung himself over, jamming his right hand into the crack. He cried out, desperately scrabbling with his right foot to obtain purchase. Eventually he was able to lodge it in the crack, and he clung to the rock, gasping convulsively. With a sudden clarity of mind, he grasped the extent of his predicament. He didn't have the strength to hold himself in the crack indefinitely—his left leg had begun to twitch spasmodically ("sewing machine leg," in the climber's vernacular) and he could no longer feel his fingers. Basically, he had two choices: get up quickly or fall.

He looked up. He thought he had about ten feet more to climb before the crack curved off to the right, at which point he thought he might be able to reach the lip of the shaft, or possibly grab on to a branch and hoist himself up. The climbing itself looked fairly straightforward, but in light of his rapidly hemorrhaging strength, he reckoned his chances were fifty-fifty at best. He resisted the temptation to wallow in either noble or maudlin sentiments. He couldn't afford to waste the energy.

He began to move up mechanically, grunting in pain with each movement of his right leg. Left foot, right hand, right foot, left hand. Tears filling his eyes. Don't think about it, keep the rhythm going, blood streaming from his knuckles now, muscles screaming. The crack slanting off to the right, he was able to stand on the lower edge now, cold spray on his face, the rock wet to touch. Reach up swimming against the current, need to breathe, his dead fingers curling over a tiny crumbling edge, shoes scraping against slimy rock, falling back. Branches breaking above, his wrist suddenly caught in a firm grip, pulling him up.

A large white face looming like a full moon. "Good God, Mr. Powell, what in heaven's name are you doing? You've scared us half to death!"

CHAPTER 19

The Stern Inquisitor, the Tender Angel of Mercy, and the Man in the Moon waxing and waning as Powell slipped in and out of consciousness. Yin and Yang, Heaven and Hell, Torment and Redemption.

Then the Man in the Moon low in the sky, shaking him. "Sorry to disturb you, Mr. Powell, but we have to wake you every hour to see if you're all right."

I'll be all right if you'll jus' let me sleep, he thought.

"Let's have a look at him, Sergeant." The Stern Inquisitor bending over and shining a light in Powell's eye. First the left, then the right. "Pupils responding normally. How's the leg?"

"He was moaning in his sleep." The Tender Angel's concerned voice.

"Here, let's have a look at it."

Powell wide-awake now. "Ouch! For God's sake, take it easy."

Dr. Harris smiling. "Back in the land of the living, are we?"

Powell looked perplexed. "What's going on?"

Harris studied his demeanor. "Why don't you tell me?"

Powell looked around the room. The curtains were parted slightly; it was dark outside. He was in his room at the Wrecker's Rest. Sergeant Black and Jane Goode stood beside his bed looking on anxiously. Dr. Harris was on the other side of the bed, face expressionless. Powell tried to think. His head throbbed and his knee ached. "The mine," he said hesitantly. "I must have had an accident."

Black cleared his throat, as if he were about to say something.

"No need to think about that now," Dr. Harris interjected. "You need to rest. One of us will check in on you from time to time."

Powell mumbled something and then closed his eyes.

"He's had a nasty time of it," Dr. Harris said, "but there shouldn't be any permanent damage. The effects of the concussion should wear off in a few days." He sipped his coffee. "Very thoughtful of your sister-in-law to put a pot on, Chief Inspector."

Butts grunted.

Dr. Harris looked at Black. "And see that he has that knee looked at."

Black smiled forlornly. "I'll do my best."

Jane Goode shook her head. "Why would anyone do it? It just doesn't make any sense."

Black's expression was deadly serious now. "Well, I'm bloody well going to find out."

Butts drew himself up in the manner of someone taking charge. "Right. According to Dr. Harris, here, Mr. Powell is going to be laid up for a day or two. Have a chat with him tomorrow morning, Black, and see if you can find out what happened." Butts glanced speculatively at Harris.

Harris sighed. "It should be all right, provided he's feeling up to it."

Butts nodded. "Then report back to me. We still have to talk to Rowlands and Jim Porter, but that can wait until we know exactly where we stand."

Black seemed about to say something but evidently thought better of it.

"Yes, sir."

"Right, then. I'm going to turn in."

There was a polite round of good-nights.

After Butts had gone, Dr. Harris turned to Black. "Do you suppose this attempt on Mr. Powell's life is in some way related to what happened to Nick Tebble?"

Black looked at him. "It would be one hell of a coincidence if it wasn't."

Harris nodded absently. "Yes—yes, I suppose so."

"May I say something now?" Jane Goode sounded a trifle annoyed.

"Yes, of course, ma'am."

"Assuming that Powell was hot on somebody's trail, what could he possibly have known that you or Buttie didn't know? It doesn't make any sense to me that a fox trying to put the hounds off his trail would gain anything by trying to kill one of the hounds. It would only intensify the chase, wouldn't it?"

"An interesting analogy, Ms. Goode," Black said. "But to carry on with your animal theme, we've all heard about the cornered rat, haven't we? You're right about one thing, though," he concluded grimly. "It'll intensify the bloody chase, all right."

* * *

The next morning Powell awoke feeling almost human. The back of his head was tender to the touch with a hint of dried blood, his knuckles were scraped, and his knee ached dully. He felt like he'd been soundly stomped in a particularly boisterous scrum. According to Jane Goode, Dr. Harris had gone home but would be looking in a little later. The highlight of his day, so far, had been Jane serving him breakfast in bed: two lightly poached eggs with a sliced tomato, a stack of dry brown toast kept warm in a linen napkin, a pot of marmalade, and a glass of freshly squeezed orange juice.

"You must be telepathic," Powell said.

"I am, actually."

Powell feigned a look of alarm.

"Relax, your secret's safe with me. If you must know, Sergeant Black has given me complete instructions on how to look after you. Feed three times daily and change paper once a week. By the way, your wife doesn't do this sort of thing for you, does she?"

"Not on your life. She's a liberated woman."

"I think I'm going to hit you with this," Jane Goode said, holding something behind her back. With a flourish, she produced a cane, a blue ribbon tied in a bow just below the crook. "I thought you might find it useful."

"Thank you, Jane. I'm truly touched to know that you think of me as frail and decrepit."

"Any more of your cheek and I'll hand you over to Mrs. Polfrock."

"I'll have you know that Mrs. Polfrock is a perfectly charming woman."

She raised an eyebrow. "You have hit your head, haven't

you?" In spite of the banter, she had been keeping a close eye on Powell. Dr. Harris had instructed her to look for any signs of confusion or other unusual behavior, but to her considerable relief, he seemed to be acting normally, at least as far as she was able to tell.

"Don't worry, Jane."

"What?"

Powell smiled. "I'm the one who's telepathic. You've been watching me out of the side of your eye ever since you came in here. I can assure you that I'm not out of my head." If I was, he thought wistfully, I'd have invited you into bed with me.

"Powell," she said hesitantly, "perhaps if I'd gone with you, as you'd asked, none of this would have happened. I—"

"Nonsense. I'm fine, honestly."

"Well, if you're sure, I'll get Sergeant Black."

"What?"

"Toodle-oo."

Powell felt slightly cheated as she left the room and Black squeezed in beside the bed to take her place.

"Good morning, sir," Black said cheerfully.

"I've had better," Powell grumbled. "What's up?"

"Er, I wanted to have a word, sir. About yesterday, about what happened out at the mine."

"That!" Powell said sheepishly. "There's not much to tell, really. I was poking around and stumbled onto an old mine shaft." Powell went on to explain how the opening had been covered by bushes and how he'd fallen through.

There was an awkward silence. "I don't think it happened quite that way, sir."

"What do you mean?" Powell asked sharply. "I was there, after all!"

"What I mean is, sir, there is evidence that someone, er, assaulted you."

"That's ridiculous! What evidence?"

"An iron pipe with blood on it, lying beside the opening. And there was blood on the back of your head, sir."

"I fell down a mine shaft, what do you expect?"

Black persisted. "I think this person struck you on the back of the head with the pipe. You fell forward, broke through the foliage, and ended up down the hole."

Powell could think of nothing to say. It was almost as if he'd known all along it had happened that way. He looked up at his colleague. "What a bloody job, eh, Bill?"

Black nodded glumly.

"It's bad enough that someone tries to kill me, then, half out of my head, I do my bloody best to finish the job. I don't know what I could have been thinking." He shook his head in disgust. "Sometimes I seriously wonder if I'm past it."

Black smiled hopefully. "All's well that ends well, sir."

"Thanks to you, Bill."

Black grinned. "Always happy to lend a hand, sir."

"Yes, well, what are we to make of it, then?"

"I was hoping you'd be able to shed some light on the matter, sir."

"Yes, I suppose—" It hit him like a load of bricks. "Porter!"

"Sir?"

"You'll remember I talked to him on the way out to the mine . . ."

Black swore violently, out of character for him. "Of course! My head mustn't be screwed on right."

"He doesn't seem the type, somehow, but we'd better have Butts pull him in for questioning. In any case, he was working beside the road; he may have seen somebody else go by."

"I'd like to talk to him, sir."

"Do you think that would be wise?"

A lengthy silence, then Black sighed heavily. "Probably not."

"Why don't you go and fetch Butts, while I rack my brain a bit."

After Black had gone, Powell threw back the duvet and struggled stiffly out of bed. He picked up his new cane from the foot of the bed and hobbled around the room in his shorts. He felt slightly dizzy at first, but the sensation soon passed. He found that if he held his right leg straight and kept his weight off it, the discomfort was bearable and he could get around quite well. He carefully lowered himself back down onto the bed and began the Herculean task of getting dressed.

A few minutes later there was a knock on the door and Butts came in with Sergeant Black close on his heels.

"Mr. Powell, what the devil are you doing?" Butts admonished.

"Don't worry, Butts. I'll answer to Dr. Harris."

"That's the least of my worries," Butts protested. "I'm only concerned with your welfare—"

"Nonsense, never felt better in my life. I'm not one for lying abed of a morning."

"But, sir—"

"Now, then, I imagine Black has already filled you in.

I'd like you to bring Jim Porter in and wring him dry. Let me know how you make out and then we can decide on the next step. Black, you can tag along to take notes."

Black beamed. "Right."

When he was alone again, Powell sat on the edge of his bed for some time recalling Black's quotation from the Scottish play. He thought about resting for a while but decided he'd be better off up and about, rather than fretting in bed about things over which he had no control. There would be plenty of time for that later, *When the hurlyburly's done, / When the battle's lost and won.*

CHAPTER 20

Powell spent the day prowling the corridors of the Wrecker's Rest and generally making a nuisance of himself. He even managed to drag Jane Goode away from her writing by playing shamelessly on her lingering feelings of guilt. He persuaded her to take him tottering down to the quay where they sat together on a bench in awkward silence amidst the sunshine and screaming gulls. Out of the blue, she said that she would be returning to London soon, to which Powell was unable to think of a reply.

Later that afternoon when Butts and Black finally returned, after what had seemed to Powell like an eternity, they found him pacing back and forth in his room like a caged animal. "What kept you so long?" he said irritably.

Butts and Black exchanged looks.

Butts cleared his throat. "Well, sir, by the time we picked Porter up and took him into St. Ives—"

"Yes?"

"Er, do you mind if we all sit down, sir?"

Powell waved impatiently. "Fine, fine." He lowered

204

himself slowly onto the edge of the bed while his colleagues pulled up chairs.

Butts sighed. "We did our best, but the poor bugger
didn't seem to know if he was coming or going."

"Could you be a little more specific?"

"Well, it's obvious that he thinks his life's a failure: his
business, if you can call it that, his marriage, his future
prospects, you name it."

"We got him to admit that it was him I saw running
from the cottage the morning Tebble was killed," Black
said. "He said that he knew his wife was with somebody
that morning, but he swears that he didn't get a chance to
find out who it was before I interrupted him."

Powell frowned. "Did you ask him if he had any
ideas?"

"Of course, sir," Butts interjected smartly, not used to
sharing the limelight. "He started raving at that point, and
Wilcox's name came up."

"Wilcox?"

"Apparently the missus told him about Wilcox coming
out that time to quote on the installation of an indoor
plumbing system, but Mr. Porter obviously wasn't buy-
ing it."

Powell frowned. "If there is some hanky-panky going
on between Linda Porter and Wilcox, why would she tell
her husband about the service call?"

Butts shrugged.

"And Rowlands?" Powell asked.

"Porter knows what's going on all right, I'm certain
of it."

"Did he mention Tebble as a possible object of his
wife's affection?"

"No, sir."

"That's interesting, don't you think, Black? Tebble's boat parked on the beach not fifty yards away."

"Well, sir, if Mr. Porter knew that it was Tebble who was, er, visiting his wife that morning, he might not mention it because of the obvious connection we'd make with Tebble's murder. He doesn't seem to have much of an alibi Saturday afternoon, by the way; he claims he was off somewhere by himself."

"Convenient," Butts muttered.

"On the other hand," Black went on, "he might be telling the truth."

Powell smiled dryly. "Thank you for clarifying that."

Butts cleared his throat. "I questioned him about the conversation he had with you yesterday morning, sir. He was a bit edgy after I told you you'd had an accident at the mine. He said he'd been upset when he talked to you, but wouldn't say much more. I asked him if he saw anybody else pass by on the road, but he claims he left a short time later to work at another location. However, there doesn't seem to be anyone who can corroborate his whereabouts."

An ominous rumble from Sergeant Black.

"That's about all we could get out of him," Butts concluded, "so we took him home and planted the thought that we might want to talk to him again."

Powell looked at Butts. "What do your instincts tell you?"

Butts considered the question for a moment. "I don't think we can rule him out at this point."

"Bill?"

"I agree with Mr. Butts," Black said diplomatically. "Porter just strikes me as being too much of a Nervous Nellie."

Powell nodded. "By the way, how did Mrs. Porter react when you showed up to pick up her husband?"

"She wasn't there. Porter claims she went to Redruth yesterday to do some shopping and visit a friend. She's due back tomorrow, apparently."

"A friend," Powell said doubtfully.

"I don't think Mr. Porter believed her, either."

"The plot thickens."

"Sir?"

"You chaps had better wander over to the Head and have that chat with Tony Rowlands. I'll stay here and sit on my arse. You can fill me in over dinner."

Several minutes later, as Powell was attempting to settle himself in bed with the latest issue of *Trout and Salmon* magazine, Black charged in, puffing like a Cape buffalo.

"It's Rowlands, sir. He's disappeared!"

The three policemen, working on their second bottles of ale, courtesy of Mrs. Polfrock, sat in the Residents' Lounge of the Wrecker's Rest discussing the implications of this latest turn of events. (Powell had his leg propped up on a large cushion, having grudgingly admitted that perhaps he *had* been overdoing it a bit.) According to Jenny Thompson, who was understandably upset, Rowlands had departed unannounced the previous evening and had yet to return. Under questioning she admitted stoically that it wasn't the first time something like this had happened. She let on that she knew about

Linda Porter, but she refused to talk about it other than to clearly indicate her disgust with Rowlands in particular, and with men in general.

"Bloody peculiar, I'd say," Butts observed. "I've already put the word out on him, by the way."

"I don't think there's much doubt about it at this point," Black agreed. "Someone pushes Mr. Powell down a mine shaft and then Rowlands disappears."

"Perhaps he's shopping in Redruth with a friend," Powell said casually.

Butts looked solemn. "Well, this is it."

After spending a restless night dreaming that someone was trying to saw his right leg off, Powell awoke to the news that Rowlands had been picked up in London and was being held in custody for questioning. At a hurriedly convened breakfast conference, it was agreed that Powell would return to London immediately to interview Rowlands, while Black stayed behind for the time being to await further developments.

Arrangements having been made, Powell was hobbling up to his room to pack when he met Jane Goode coming down the stairs. He had been dreading this moment, but he supposed it was as good a time as any.

She looked at him sternly. "You really should stay off that leg, you know."

"Jane, there's been a break in the case. I have to return to London today, and I wanted to say goodbye . . . I mean, well, to wish you luck with your book—"

"Nonsense! I'll come with you and you can tell me all about it. I was planning on leaving tomorrow, myself, but what the hell? We can keep each other company."

Powell grinned like a rustic on market day. "Great! The InterCity leaves Redruth at ten-oh-nine, and we should be there at least fifteen minutes early—can you be ready in half an hour?"

A look of panic as she glanced at her watch. "Good Lord!" She dashed back up the stairs.

A half hour later, after a last minute conversation with Butts and a disconcertingly cordial goodbye from Mrs. Polfrock, Powell and Jane squeezed into the backseat of the car behind Sergeant Black.

"Ow! Get your hand off my knee!" Powell yelped.

Jane laughed unsympathetically. "Sorry."

During an uneventful drive to Redruth, Powell brought Jane up to date, then Black dropped them off at the station.

"Thanks, Bill. I'll let you know."

"Good luck, Mr. Powell. And goodbye, Ms. Goode. I'll keep my eye out for your new book."

"Don't hold your breath. But you can still buy a copy of my first one," she said hopefully.

Black grinned. "I already have. I picked up a copy in Truro. I found it quite interesting. I'd like to discuss it with you sometime."

She shook her head in amazement. "If I ever get around to writing a mystery, I'll call it *Death and the Literary Sergeant* and dedicate it to you. And do give me a call; I'd like that."

"If you two are quite finished," Powell said, "we've a train to catch."

They waved as Black drove off. A few minutes later they were sitting together in their coach, strangely silent.

It wasn't until the train was pulling out of the station that Jane Goode spoke.

"It's a funny old life, isn't it?"

"Didn't Margaret Thatcher say that when they stuck the knife in?"

She stared straight ahead. "I went to Penrick to write a book, ended up getting involved in a murder and falling for a man with a cane."

Powell stunned. "Jane, I—"

"Don't pay any attention to me, I find this sort of thing cathartic." She turned to look at him. "I imagine you're happily married . . ."

He looked into her eyes and only barely managed a smile. "You've been taking lessons from Mrs. Polfrock."

"It's none of my business, I know."

"It's all right . . ." He hesitated. "I don't know, I don't normally think about marriage in those terms."

"That's hardly a ringing endorsement of the institution."

He looked away. "I guess what I'm trying to say is, I'm not the easiest person to live with. My wife has to put up with a lot. I tend to get . . . preoccupied with things."

"So I've noticed."

"I'm flattered, Jane, I really am. I want you to know that I find you very attractive and I wish . . . the thing is, I'm not in a position to—"

"I can assure you that I'm not in the habit of chasing after married men either." There was something in her voice.

He looked at her, concern in his eyes. "Jane, I didn't mean—"

She sighed. "I know." There was a lengthy silence. "But old Maggie was right. Who can say why things turn out the way they do? Is it predetermination or simply random chance that one chooses a particular path or meets a particular person? And does it really matter in the end?"

Powell assumed that the questions were intended to be rhetorical so he stared out the window. An endless procession of power poles and fields flashed by, and an ominous-looking cooling tower in the distance like some high-tech scarecrow. Amidst the rhythmic clattering of the wheels and the gentle swaying of the coach, the sound of his breathing, the comforting pressure of Jane's arm against his, he was soon asleep.

A bright voice roused him. "We're here."

He looked up groggily into Jane's smiling face. "What time is it?"

"Nearly three. I didn't want to wake you."

Powell looked out the window at the familiar surroundings of Paddington Station.

"We'd better get off," Jane was saying. "Here's your stick. I'll take your bag."

There was an awkward moment as they stood together on the crowded platform.

"Take care of yourself, Powell."

"You, too."

She pressed something into his hand, her fingers warm and probing. A piece of paper. "My phone number—for Sergeant Black. He wanted to talk to me about my book."

"Yes, of course."

"Goodbye."

His goodbye was still on his lips as she slipped into the stream of passersby.

He made his way slowly outside and hailed a cab.

CHAPTER 21

When Powell arrived at the Yard, he had to endure the inevitable cracks about the cane and his general state of decrepitude as he limped to his office. "Bloody touching," he remarked to Inspector Richards as he slumped into his chair. His desk was uncharacteristically neat and tidy, like a fallow field of simulated wood grain plastic laminate waiting to be sown with paper. He looked around the office. Everything was as he'd left it. Drab metal bookshelves and file cabinets, and in keeping with the Metropolitan Police Green Plan, not a trace of endangered hardwoods anywhere. Another of Sir Henry Merriman's P.C. initiatives (Politically Constipated, to the rank and file). Powell grimaced.

"It looks painful, sir," Richards said eventually.

Powell ignored him. "How's our pigeon?"

"Ready to go whenever you are."

"Any indications?"

Richards yawned. It wasn't his case so he wasn't particularly interested. "We told him we wanted to question him about the murder of Nick Tebble. He's been cautioned but hasn't shown any interest in calling a lawyer. He seems a bit jumpy. If he's got something to hide, it's my guess he'll sing."

Do pigeons sing? Powell wondered. "Did he say what he was doing in London?"

"Claims he's been working too hard and needed a break."

"I don't bloody doubt it. You'd better come along to keep me from throttling the bugger."

A sudden look of alarm flickered across Richards's face. "Yes, sir." The young up-and-coming inspector took himself very seriously.

"And I'd like you to take notes."

"Sir?" An "I don't do windows" sort of expression.

Powell glared at him. "Yes, Richards?"

Inspector Richards sighed. "Very good, sir."

Rowlands was waiting in the interview room, watched over by a fresh-faced constable. He twisted around awkwardly in his tiny chair as Powell and Inspector Richards walked in. An attempt to suppress the look of alarm on his face failed, but he said nothing.

Not a poker player, Powell thought. He dismissed the constable and pulled up a chair opposite Rowlands, placing his cane carefully on the table. Richards sat in the corner behind Rowlands, fiddling with his notebook.

"Surprised to see me, Tony?" Powell said evenly.

Rowlands's large face was moist with perspiration. He refused to meet Powell's eye. "I heard you had an accident." His voice brittle.

"Somebody pushed me down a mine shaft, if that's what you're referring to."

There was panic in Rowlands's eyes. "Pushed? What do you mean? I was at the pub, ask Jenny!" He looked almost comically earnest.

Powell smiled. "Good heavens. I've only asked one question and you've already raised so many interesting points. First off, when did you say you were at the pub?"

"Tuesday afternoon. There were customers that must have seen me." Rowlands was sweating profusely now.

"Tuesday afternoon?" A pregnant pause.

"Yeah, well I bumped into old George that evening, didn't I? He told me that you'd, er, had an accident at the mine."

"George?"

"Polfrock."

"Oh, yes, one of your best customers, I understand."

Rowlands spoke very carefully. "He comes in for a drink now and then. When the old lady lets him out, that is."

"Is that where you bumped into old George, at the pub?"

"Yeah, why don't you ask Jenny?" A trace of belligerence in his voice now.

"Ah, yes, Jenny. Her name does seem constantly to come up in relation to your whereabouts."

"We work together, don't we?"

Powell smirked. "What else do you do together, Tony?"

"That's none of your business," Rowlands answered indignantly.

"It's your alibi, not mine."

"Alibi? What do you mean?"

Powell stared at Rowlands without replying. He had seen and heard enough to come to some conclusions. Thick as a plank but possessed, no doubt, with a certain measure of cunning when it came to preserving his own skin. But a killer? He reached under the table and gently massaged his knee. He was trying to keep an open mind. In any case, he decided that subtlety would be wasted on Rowlands—best to let him have it with both barrels, although it could prove to be a difficult shot. "Tony," he said suddenly, "what does Linda Porter think about Jenny working under you?"

For a moment Powell was concerned that he'd have to leap over the table and administer mouth-to-mouth resuscitation. Rowlands had turned a ghastly shade of purple and was sputtering apoplectically, his thick lips flecked with spittle.

Powell was mildly relieved a few seconds later when Rowlands motioned frantically for the water pitcher at the far end of the table. "Richards, get Mr. Rowlands a glass of water, would you?"

Richards sauntered over grudgingly, poured a glass from the carafe, and handed it to Rowlands.

Rowlands guzzled it greedily. His demeanor gradually returned to a semblance of normality.

"I know about you and Linda, Tony, so there's no point in denying it. I also know about your little smuggling operation. And finally," he lied, "I know all about Nick Tebble. Why don't you come clean and save us both a lot of trouble?"

"You can't keep a secret in that sodding town," Rowlands muttered. Then he was silent for a considerable length of time and one could almost hear the wheels turning. He looked at Powell, eyes narrowing. "What's in it for me?" he asked.

"That depends on what you've done, doesn't it?"

"Well, I never killed anybody—never even tried to," he added quickly.

"Well, that's a start. You know that you're free to contact a solicitor at any time?" Powell said, crossing his fingers.

Rowlands sighed heavily. "Ask me anything you want. I've got nothing to lose anymore. I just want some bloody peace of mind. You don't know what it's been like living with what I've had to live with all these years."

Powell pushed off the safety. It was a straightaway shot, after all, but he'd let his bird sing awhile before he pulled the trigger. "Why don't you start at the beginning?"

"It was nineteen-sixty-six and I'd just moved to Penrick and set myself up as a publican. I'd, er, made a bit of money in London, small-time stuff, you understand, enough for a down payment on the Head. I was mortgaged up to my balls, but I needed to establish myself as a respectable member of the community and get to know the lay of the land." He lowered his voice. "I was doing this drug deal, see. Half a ton of cannabis resin. I'd been planning it for years. I had this mate who could get the stuff from Morocco to Gibraltar, load it onto a yacht, then run it into the Channel. Then we'd switch it over to a fishing boat off Land's End and unload it at some secluded cove along the Cornish coast. Penrick seemed like the ideal base of operations."

Sing, birdie, sing.

"I settled on Mawgawan Beach early on. It was much more private in those days. You'd get the odd adventurous type camping out there in the summer, but that was about it. The thing about Mawgawan Beach is you can get a sizable boat in there safely at night. But the problem was getting the goods off the beach. There's no way up the cliffs there; the nearest place to get the stuff out is the Old Fish Cellar."

"That's where Nick Tebble comes into it." Stating the obvious with a knowing air of nonchalance rarely failed to impress. Merriman had made a career of it.

Rowlands nodded ruefully. "Christ, if I'd only known what I was getting myself into."

"He was a bit of an eccentric, I understand," Powell remarked sympathetically.

An edgy laugh. "Eccentric? He was eccentric all right. The thing was, I needed somebody who could handle a small boat and knew the local waters to ferry the goods from Mawgawan Beach to someplace safe. Like I said, the Old Fish Cellar seemed perfect. The place is fairly isolated, and I'd learned that Tebble lived alone and knew his way around boats."

"How did you approach Tebble in the first place?"

"He came into the Head one night and I started chatting him up, you know how it is. Served him a couple on the house after closing time. He started coming in every night after that. He had a thing about foreigners—anyone not from Cornwall, that is—and was always going on about how hard done by the Cornish were. It was Cousin Jack *this* and Cousin Jack *that*. It was enough to make you puke. But I went along with it to get on the right side of him. It wasn't long before I had him eating out of my hand." He frowned. "Or so I thought. To cut a long story short, I finally put it to him one night: fifty thousand quid, free and clear, if he did his bit and kept his mouth shut."

That explained the money. "I'm a little puzzled—what made you think he could be trusted?"

"It was obvious that he was a complete nutter. I reckoned if he squealed no one would believe him. It would be his word against mine, me a pillar of the community. It turned out that I underestimated him."

"What do you mean?"

"He was a raving bloody psychotic, that's what," Rowlands replied petulantly, as if Tebble's mental condition, whatever it might have been, was a personal affront to himself. An errant comet orbiting around his sun.

"Would you care to elaborate?" Powell held his breath, the gun firmly seated against his shoulder now.

Rowlands's eyes were almost pleading. "If I tell you what happened, will you go easy on me? Like I said, I never hurt anybody . . ."

"But I think you have, Tony. All the kids who smoked that hash, for instance. Who knows how they all ended up?"

"That was thirty years ago!" Rowlands exclaimed.

Powell regarded him placidly. "If you cooperate, it will be taken into account, I can promise you that. In any case, I think you need to get it off your chest."

Rowlands took his head in his hands and moaned. "What I wouldn't give for thirty years of peace and quiet to make up for the thirty years of hell I've been through."

Maybe not thirty years, Powell thought, but we'll do our best. Inspector Richards was yawning in the corner,

which was annoyingly distracting under the circumstances. Powell flashed him a withering look. "Well, how
about it, Tony?"

Rowlands began to speak in a monotone, like someone
had pulled the cord on one of those talking dolls. "It was
April eleventh, nineteen-sixty-seven. I remember it like it
was yesterday. It was a moonless night—overcast, like—
and the tides were just right. The whole thing went off
without a hitch. The plan was to keep the goods at the
Old Fish Cellar for two weeks then transport them by
lorry to Birmingham for distribution." Rowlands shook
his head in disgust. "But then Nick started running off at
the mouth. He'd get into his cups and go on and on about
the good old days—the wrecking and the smuggling.
Christ Almighty! I had to shut him up more than once. It
got to the point where I could no longer trust him. I mean
I didn't think he'd nark on me on purpose—not if he
wanted to get paid—I was more afraid he might let something slip that would point the finger to the Old Fish
Cellar. To be on the safe side, I decided we'd better move
the goods somewhere else until my mate in Birmingham
was ready for them. I told Nick about it and gave the
impression that it was all part of the plan. Fair-traders
like us can't be too careful, nudge, nudge—you get the
idea. So we moved the goods up to the mine one night
and stashed them down one of the old shafts. I told Nick
to keep an eye on the place until we was ready to ship
them out." A strange expression clouded his features.
"You don't know how much I've come to regret that
decision."

Powell stared at him. "Not as much as Ruth Trevenney."

CHAPTER 22

Powell listened with an odd sense of detachment as the story unfolded. The events surrounding the murder of Ruth Trevenney, as Rowlands related them, were startling, yet not unexpected, a bit like one's first glimpse of the wild Cornish coast she had loved so well.

It seemed that Nick Tebble had taken his role as guardian of their drug stash extremely seriously. According to Rowlands, Tebble encountered Ruth at the mine one afternoon picking wildflowers. In the grip of some paranoid delusion, he forced her down one of the old adits, raped her, then slit her throat.

"He didn't say anything to me about it until after the body had washed up on the Sands a few days later. The thing is," Rowlands said in a hollow voice, eyes averted, "the bastard was proud of himself." He looked up at Powell. "Whatever else I might have done in my time, I've no stomach for murder. I was completely shattered by what Nick had done. I even thought about chucking the whole operation. But then I figured I'd better go through with it so I could set myself up for life, respectable like, and not have to get involved in that kind of dodge again."

Powell was thinking about Roger Trevenney. "Did it ever occur to you to go to the police?" he asked sharply.

"I figured I was in it too deep. Considering that Nick was two pence short of a bob, I was scared they'd try to hang Ruth's murder on me. Perhaps if I had . . ." He left it hanging.

If wishes were horses, Powell thought. "Go on."

Rowlands shrugged. "Not much more to tell, really. I did the deal, we all got paid and lived unhappily ever after."

Irony, Powell marveled; perhaps I've underestimated old Tony. "When did Tebble start blackmailing you?"

"You don't miss a thing, do you?"

Rhetorical questions, even.

"He was all right for a few months," Rowlands continued, "then he started up again. He wanted me to plan another operation." He shook his head. "It's not like he needed to work. I told him to piss off, but he wouldn't get off it, threatened to blow the gaff if I didn't play along. You see, Nick was handy with the practical things, but he didn't have a head for planning. That's why he needed me."

Powell was puzzled. "Did you ever consider calling his bluff? Tebble had more to lose than you by going to the police."

"You didn't know him—he didn't think like a normal bloke. He was like a kamikaze pilot. Looking back on it now, I suppose I could've bolted and hoped for the best, but at the time I figured I'd be better off sticking around so I could keep an eye on him. In the end we settled on a small-time operation, running goods over from France every couple of months or so—wine, cigarettes, that sort of thing. It was fairly low risk, there was no shortage of local customers, and I figured it would keep Nick busy and out of trouble."

"I understand that George Polfrock is a client of yours."

Rowlands looked surprised then smirked. "Yeah, our George is quite a reader."

"When did your little business arrangement with Tebble start to fall apart?"

"About a month ago. He came to the Head one night after closing time and told me he was tired of pissing around with booze and dirty books, he wanted to do something really big, another drug deal like the one we'd done in the Sixties. I refused flat out, of course, but once again he wouldn't take no for an answer." His expression hardened. "A short time later your Riddle turned up— Nick's little reminder for me about Ruth Trevenney, as if I needed one."

"How did he pull it off?"

Rowlands explained how a body had washed up on the beach at the Old Fish Cellar one day; Tebble had seen his opportunity and taken advantage of it. Tebble had been fascinated by his luminous woodpile and twigged to the idea of rigging the corpse to create a supernatural effect. When it got dark, he'd ferry it from the Old Fish Cellar to the Sands in his tiny skiff, unload it on the beach halfway between the village and Towey Head, scatter bits of the fungus all over it, then hide out in the Towans until someone out for an evening stroll happened along. After his victim had fled the scene, he'd load the body back in his boat and head for home. During the day he kept it packed in salt in his cellar.

"No one ever reported seeing a boat," Powell interjected.

"He used a wagon of some sort to lug it into the towans. And sometimes when the tide was out he used it to haul the body to and from his skiff."

Powell nodded, satisfied. Now a shot in the dark.

"Do you know anything about Ruth's diary?"

Rowlands looked puzzled. "Didn't know she had one."

Powell told him about his last conversation with Roger Trevenney.

Rowlands smiled grimly. "Nick was capable of doing whatever it took to get his way. He told me he was going to talk to Trevenney. Threatening to tip him off was Nick's way of turning up the pressure."

"He never actually got around to it though, did he, Tony? Because somebody killed him. Somebody with something to gain, or at least nothing more to lose?"

Fear in his eyes now. "Look, Chief Superintendent, I've been straight with you up to now but—" He choked off the words. He sounded desperate. "I need to think."

Powell spoke slowly:

> *"Come, you spirits*
> *That tend on mortal thoughts, unsex me here,*
> *And fill me, from the crown to the toe, top-full*
> *Of direst cruelty! Make thick my blood . . ."*

Rowlands looked befuddled. "What did you say?"

"She's just like Lady Macbeth, isn't she, Tony?"

It took a moment to sink in, then an expression of awe

on Rowlands's face. "Gawd! Is there anything you don't know?"

Inspector Richards in the corner suppressed a snort.

"Why don't you tell me about you and Linda?" Powell said.

Rowlands laughed bitterly. "You've seen her, the bloody bitch exudes sex. I've always had a weakness for the ladies, and when she and that nancy-boy husband of hers rented one of my cottages, well, one thing led to another. I only wanted a bit of fun, but it was clear she was looking for a way out of her situation." A slight hesitation. "I might have led her on a bit. You see, I've always planned to retire to Spain—I've got a villa out there—and I, uh, promised to take her with me someday."

Powell regarded him with distaste. "Was that your intention?"

"Come on, Chief Superintendent, you and I are both men of the world. I like a nice bit of crumpet as well as the next bloke, but I'm not bloody crazy."

"What did Jenny think of this arrangement?"

"Jenny? Why should she care—"

"Cut the crap, Tony!" Powell snapped.

Rowlands looked sheepish. "Jenny is, er, not the jealous type."

"Perhaps I'll ask her myself."

"She's known me for a long time . . . I mean, she knows what I'm like," Rowlands said weakly, as if that explained everything.

"Tell me more about Linda."

"After the Riddle started, I found that I was spending more and more time with her. My nerves were shot, and I needed someone to talk to. I told her about the drugs, about Nick, Ruth Trevenney, everything. She seemed very understanding, very protective." He looked at Powell, his face expressionless.

"What about her husband? Did he know about the two of you?"

"I've no idea. Even if he had, I don't imagine he would have done anything about it."

"How did you and Linda manage your liaisons?"

"Jim has been reduced to taking odd jobs at various local farms to make ends meet. Linda would let me know when he'd be away for the day; I'd pick her up at the top of the lane and we'd drive to an abandoned farmhouse I know of."

"Were you with Linda at her cottage last Saturday, the day Tebble was murdered?"

"No, I just told you we never did it there."

"She said she was with you."

A look of panic on his face. "I told her I couldn't— look, it's not true, I promise you!"

"Well she was with somebody that morning, and it wasn't Mr. Porter. Any idea who it was?"

"What do you mean, *with* somebody?"

"You're a man of the world, Tony. Use your imagination."

The publican seemed to be sulking, which was rather ludicrous under the circumstances, Powell thought. "There was a small dinghy on the beach near the cottage," he persisted.

Rowlands suddenly turned white as a sheet. He looked like he was going to be sick. For several seconds, he seemed incapable of speaking. Eventually he managed a hoarse whisper. "Good Christ, she not only shoved a spade in his guts, she screwed the poor bastard first!"

The rest of Rowlands's account seemed almost anticlimactic. He had told Linda Porter about Tebble's intention to go to Trevenney. She had tried to convince him to do something about it then threatened to take matters into her own hands (to protect her investment, Powell surmised). In the end, it appeared that she had resorted to her considerable charms, of which Tebble had evidently availed himself, to try and persuade old Nick to be reasonable. Offering her body to someone like Tebble could only be viewed as an act of desperation, but regardless of what transpired between them in her cottage that day, she ended up following him back to the Old Fish Cellar where she killed him.

Bang, bang. Two birds in the bag at last. There were still a few loose ends, not the least of which was the identity of the person who had tried to send him on a one-way trip down a mine shaft. Rowlands claimed to know nothing about it, but it was significant, Powell thought, that when he learned about the incident from George Polfrock, he had panicked and tried to put as many miles as he could between himself and Penrick. He maintained that he'd simply had enough. More likely, he was afraid that he'd be next. Rowlands knew Linda Porter better than most.

The most plausible scenario, Powell surmised, was that Jim Porter had told his wife about their encounter on the road; she had followed him up to the mine, found him in a vulnerable position, and let him have it on the head with a length of pipe. Nothing but grief in this bloody job. It didn't make a lot of sense when you thought about it, though. Kill one copper and a dozen more spring up to take his or her place. Powell supposed that she had associated the mine workings with the murder of Ruth Trevenney and her lover's role in it and had reacted irrationally, thinking perhaps that he was onto something. In any case, she was no doubt far away by now.

After they'd seen to Rowlands, Powell limped back to his office accompanied by Inspector Richards, who walked slowly and with exaggerated precision so that Powell could keep up, giving the impression that he was putting himself out.

"That was easy," Richards said smugly.

Powell stopped suddenly and glared at his subordinate. "Get stuffed, Richards, and when you've done that, type up your notes. I want them on my desk in an hour."

It was nearly nine o'clock when Powell finished up. He'd just got off the phone to Sergeant Black in Penrick, having set the wheels in motion. He thought about the rest of his evening, such as it was. Marion and the boys wouldn't be back until Sunday and he didn't relish the thought of a frozen dinner alone in his empty house. He reached into his pocket and extracted a crumpled piece of paper. He unfolded it carefully. Jane Goode's phone number. He picked up the telephone and began to press the keys. After the first few digits he paused, then he slowly replaced the receiver in its cradle. He reached into a desk drawer for an envelope, placed the paper inside, and sealed it. He got up stiffly and put on his jacket. He picked up his cane and made his way into the outer office. There was a bank of mail compartments on the wall to the right of his office door. He walked over and stuffed the envelope into the box labeled DET.-SGT. W. BLACK.

Downstairs there was a minor commotion at the reception desk. Two young women in regulation club gear—satin T-shirts, plastic miniskirts, and platform shoes—were giving the sergeant on duty a hard time. Screaming obscenities at him, to be more precise. From what he was able to gather, as he limped toward the door, their dates were being detained somewhere for disorderly conduct, the lot of them high on the latest designer drug by the sound of it. Nothing but grief, he thought again.

Powell stepped out into the drizzle and hailed a cab.

"Where to, guv?"

"The K2 Tandoori in Charlotte Street."

The cab sped off, tires swishing, down the rain-slicked street.

EPILOGUE

It was a little more than a week later when Powell learned that Linda Porter had been apprehended in Australia. Fought like a bloody badger, according to Sergeant Black, who had spoken with the arresting officer. After the incident at the mine, she had apparently come to the conclusion that Rowlands was a lost cause and had managed to skip the country before they'd got the word out on her. The day after she arrived back in England to begin her glacial progression through the criminal justice system, Powell received a phone call from Dr. Harris informing him that Roger Trevenney had passed away.

On the domestic front, the Powell household had returned to its usual state of chaos, which Powell found oddly comforting for a change. He was still taking a course of physiotherapy for stretched ligaments in his knee and had even managed to persuade Marion to consider another destination besides Cornwall for their family holiday that summer.

Powell had more or less put the Penrick business behind him (although he occasionally wondered how

Jane Goode was getting on) when, a few months later, he received a large, flat package from Roger Trevenney's solicitor. There was a small envelope attached with cello-tape to the brown paper wrapping. He looked at the package for a considerable length of time and then got up and closed the door to his office. He carefully removed the envelope and opened it, finding a small piece of note-paper inside. *Erskine, I wanted you to have this. Roger.*

He didn't remember removing the wrapping paper, only staring in wonder at the painting lying on his desk. A girl in a white dress, spring flowers, and the immutable sea. He sat down, lit a cigarette, and exhaled a cloud of smoke that settled slowly over the image like a Cornish mist.